FANTASY
ENCYCLOPEDIA

FANTASY
ENCYCLOPEDIA

JUDY ALLEN

KINGFISHER

KINGFISHER

Kingfisher Publication Plc
New Penderel House
283–288 High Holborn
London WC1V 7HZ
www.kingfisherpub.com

First published by Kingfisher Publications Plc
in 2005

10 9 8 7 6 5 4 3 2 1

1TR/0705/SNPLFG/CLSN(CLSN)/140MA/C

Senior editor: Carron Brown
Senior designer: Jane Tassie
Picture research manager: Cee Weston-Baker
DTP manager: Nicky Studdart
Senior production controller: Lindsey Scott
Artwork archivist: Wendy Allison
Proofreaders: Sheila Clewley, Caitlin Doyle
Additional text and indexer: Carron Brown

Judy Allen's website:
www.judyallen.co.uk

The publisher cannot be held responsible
for changes in website addresses or content.

ISBN-13: 978 0 7534 1087 5
ISBN-10: 0 7534 1087 7

Printed in China

Special thanks
*The author and publisher would
like to thank John Howe and
Tamlyn Francis for all their
help and enthusiasm.*

Contents

Foreword

Warning: the creatures in this book are real. Well, okay, maybe not physically — don't expect to find a bunyip in your bathtub or a hobgoblin under the bed. If you comb the woods for a sasquatch, the best you'll get for your trouble is a tuft of hair caught on a twig — and that might belong to anything. But make no mistake. They're real, all right. And when you read their stories, they'll come to you.

I should know. I left a door to my imagination open when I was very young and they all got in. They're still there now: fairies, dragons, vampires, genies — all jostling for position inside my head.

Fantasy sometimes scared me, but it mostly made me soar. Between the ages of seven and ten I was often ill, and spent a lot of time in bed. Once I was off school for a whole term. Reading was all I could do, and I read a lot. Not stories about real life, mind — I wanted escape. I wanted things that took me away from my dull little room and my wheezing chest. I wanted myths and monsters, I wanted flying horses to carry me to distant lands. And fantasy obliged.

Pegasus came and whisked me away — to the Cyclops' cave, to the sorcerous palaces of Arabia, to Baba Yaga's terrifying forest hut. I sought great treasures, vast knowledge, true love, eternal life. I met many of the creatures in this book and learned how to deal with them. Some should be befriended (despite their strangeness), while others can be tamed. With some you can bargain; the very worst must be fought and destroyed. There are rules for each one, and they are worth knowing. Taken together, they draw on all our endurance, courage, intelligence, compassion — the finest qualities that make us human.

I got better. I went back to school. I grew up. Got a job. But the wonders I had seen stayed with me — I glimpsed them as I sat at my desk, or walked through crowded London streets. And in the end, I couldn't ignore their call. I began writing my own stories, with my own versions of genies, imps, water spirits and dragons… This is how the creatures of fantasy have survived for thousands of years — passing from one person to another, always evolving, ever changing. And now they're heading your way too.

Let this book be your guide — the key to their mysteries. Open it on any page, and you'll find something to enchant you. It describes the shadowy, slippery inhabitants of fantasy and suggests where you might find them; even better, it tells you the rules of engagement — silver bullets and all.

This extraordinary encyclopedia is a portal to another world. Step on through and be amazed!

Jonathan Stroud,
author of The Bartimaeus Trilogy

What is fantasy?

Defining the word 'fantasy' is rather like catching fog in a fishing net. Fantasy is fluid and ever-changing, with no fixed boundaries. Its worlds drift in and out of our world, always close by, but often visible only to the imagination. Within it are myths, legends, fables and folklore, although these also exist outside it. It includes magic — both the natural enchantment of elves, fairies and spirit-beings, and the more scientific magic used by human magicians. Trying to define fantasy by its opposite does not help. The opposite of fantasy is reality — yet to say that fantasy is unreal is to imply that it does not exist, and clearly it does. Certainly between the covers of this book, each fabulous beast, each magical being, every ghost and spirit and vampire exists, with its own energy and its own power. Outside the book — readers must decide.

The very forms of the creatures and beings within fantasy are changeable. Many are shape-shifters: djinn who can become smoke or mist; men who can turn into wolves; vampires who can as easily have the bodies of bats as of humans; forest spirits who may be as tall as the tallest tree or as small as a blade of grass. And very many of them have different aspects. One of these is the triple-goddess who can appear as a young girl, a grown woman or an aged hag, and who can be innocent or nurturing or vengeful depending on her mood. Another is the dragon of the East who can as easily bring the rain that makes plants grow as the rain that causes devastating floods.

Arranging the various beings and creatures into groups for the sake of this book was difficult. They watch as you write about them — looming and hovering — and you know they do not like to be pinned down and trapped.

In the end, decisions had to be made, and here they are — although I have to say that each time I close the book and then open it up again I half expect to find the dragons and giant birds have flown and the rest have drifted onto different pages.

Judy Allen

NOTE TO READERS

This book includes historical creatures of fantasy from folklore, legends and fables. Book and film panels throughout will guide you to fictional characters, such as hobbits, and fictional worlds, such as Narnia.

Few humans see fairies or hear
their music, but many find fairy
rings of dark grass, scattered with
toadstools, left by their dancing feet.

The Little People

Elves, fairies, dwarves, goblins and their kind have

been written and spoken of in every part of the world

for centuries. They have many names, in many

languages, but prefer to be called The Strangers,

The Good Neighbours or The Little People.

They can be gentle and generous or dark and

dangerous — but even the friendliest are unreliable.

Elves and fairies

Elves have been known to humans for more than 2,000 years. They are far older than fairies. In medieval Europe, a fairy was a human woman with magical powers. It was a few hundred years before the word 'fairy' was also used to describe elves. The image of fairies with gauzy wings did not appear until the late 18th century CE. Now, either word is used for the Little People of the woods and fields.

Some elves are tiny, but others are tall, and elfin women can occasionally seem human. Seen from behind, though, they have no backs and are hollow, like a hollow tree.

Different fairies

Trooping fairies, such as the Patu-Paiarehe of the Maoris, New Zealand, live in trees and appear in mists. Like elves everywhere they love music and dancing. They will sometimes teach humans to work magic, but if they call from far off, any who follow risk becoming lost in the woods.

Some fairies are solitary, such as leprechauns. They are very rich, and humans may try to persuade a leprechaun to lead the way across meadows and marshes to his secret store of gold. He will always trick them into looking away, whereupon he will vanish, leaving them lost, bewildered and with no treasure.

The leprechaun is the fairy shoemaker of Ireland whose tapping hammer gives away his presence.

When blackberry-picking, always leave a few for the Little People.

Fairies and humans

In stories, good fairies bring blessings and help, though there are often conditions attached. Cinderella must be home by midnight or her beautiful dress will turn to rags. A farmer, paid by the fairies for help or provisions must not look at the money till he gets home or it will turn to dead leaves. Then again, he may be paid in dead leaves, which will turn to gold when he reaches home.

Pixies, who are tiny, always young and dressed in green, will help humans, especially if they are poor or are being mistreated by others. However, they can be tricky and mischievous if annoyed or not properly rewarded. In fact, to be pixie-led means to be lost.

Many Little People appreciate a tribute or gift. Traditionally, people put out a little bread from a new loaf or, when the cows are being milked, allow a little milk to run on the ground for the Little People to take.

Fairies in books and films

📖 *The Complete Book of the Flower Fairies*
Cicely Mary Barker

📖 *Peter Pan*
J M Barrie

📖 *The Little People: Stories of Fairies, Pixies and Other Small Folk*
Neil Philip

🎥 *Hook* (1991)

🎥 *The Last Leprechaun* (1998)

Traps and tricks

*I*n early folklore, the elves, though beautiful and sometimes generous, are treated with nervous respect. They are intrigued by humans but, being quick, small and supernatural, can always outwit them. Elves will steal cows, bread, milk, and also babies, who they bring up as their own, leaving a changeling, or elf-child, in its place.

KIDNAP!

Elvish women are sometimes attracted to young mortal men and may lure them into a fairy ring from which it is difficult to escape. Then, too, when elves have taken a human baby, they may try to kidnap a mortal woman to care for the child.

TIME IN FAIRYLAND

It is said to be possible for mortal men and women to spend time in fairyland and still get safely home, but only if they do not eat or drink anything while they are there. A single mouthful of fairy food and a mortal is theirs forever.

People who escape fairyland find time is different than in their own world — one hour in fairyland can be many years of human time.

LIGHT AND DARK ELVES

The light elves live in the air or in trees, and are usually kind. The dark elves, who live underground, are inclined to play malicious tricks and can make people ill just by breathing on them.

All elves have the power to use 'glamour' or enchantment to make themselves invisible. A fairy market can be seen from a distance easily, but disappears as a human draws near. Walk through it and you will be jostled and bumped as you would if you walked unseeing through a human market. Once home, you are likely to find you have become lame or ill.

Flint arrowheads, turned up by the plough, were once believed to be elf-shot, the spent weapons of the elves, whose victims would suffer illness or disability.

In their more playful moments elves spend the night twisting the hair of humans or the manes of horses, and the tangles they leave are known as elf-locks.

Elves enjoy teasing humans and laugh at their confusion.

TRICKSTERS

In German, one word for nightmare is *alpdrücken*, which translates as 'elf-pressure', because it was thought that elves sit on their victims' chests all night.

The music of the Elf-king, played on a fiddle, can sometimes be heard seeping up through the ground. If a human plays the same tune, anyone and anything that hears it will be forced to dance until the poor fiddler can play the tune backwards or someone can cut the fiddle strings.

ELVES IN BOOKS AND FILMS

📖 *Elf Hill*
Hans Christian Andersen

📖 *The Various*
Steve Augarde

📖 *The Changeling*
Malachy Doyle

🎬 *Elf* (2003)

Celebrated fairies

The most celebrated fairies are found in literature — in folk tales and fairy tales, in French medieval romances and in some of Shakespeare's plays. Some have names — including Oberon, Titania and Puck. Others are known only by title — the Tooth Fairy, who leaves coins in exchange for lost teeth, or the Fairy Godmother, who brings good fortune and grants wishes.

Robin Goodfellow, also known as Puck, is the son of Oberon, King of the Fairies, and a mortal woman. His father gave him the power to shape-shift, create illusions and cast spells. He is the most mischievous of the hobgoblins and the best at leading travellers astray.

OBERON AND TITANIA

Oberon, King of the Fairies, first appeared in a French Romantic poem, *Huon de Bordeaux*, written in the 13th or 14th century CE. The inspiration for Oberon probably came from Germany and tales of the Dwarf-King Elberich or Albrich.

Later, in the 16th century, Oberon and his queen, Titania, appeared in *A Midsummer Night's Dream*, a play by William Shakespeare (1564–1616). In Shakespeare's day, fairies were believed to be the same as the nymphs who followed the Roman moon-goddess Diana, and Titania is another name for Diana. Although this fairy king and queen are invented beings, everything they do is in keeping with elvish tradition.

Not all sightings of fairies are genuine. In 1917, in the village of Cottingley in England, two children created fake photographs of themselves with fairies. They convinced many adults, including the writer of the Sherlock Holmes detective novels, Sir Arthur Conan Doyle (1859–1930). Not until they were old ladies did one of them finally confess.

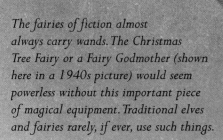

FAIRY GODMOTHERS

They appear in Greek and Roman mythology as the Fates. In Scandinavian mythology, they are Nornir or Norns. There are three of them and some say they plan human destiny, others that they merely foretell it. Certainly they spin out the thread of each human life, and when they cut the thread, that life is ended.

After much retelling of the Nornir myths, the women were described as fairies who visit each newborn baby and announce what the future holds for the child. Then came the belief that they brought gifts to the child at birth — not material things, but good fortune, talents and abilities. They became known as Fairy Godmothers, and in some tales there are seven of them, or 12, or even more.

As they changed through the years, so did their behaviour — Cinderella was not a baby but a young woman when her Fairy Godmother first came to her aid.

The fairies of fiction almost always carry wands. The Christmas Tree Fairy or a Fairy Godmother (shown here in a 1940s picture) would seem powerless without this important piece of magical equipment. Traditional elves and fairies rarely, if ever, use such things.

19

Household helpers

S ome Little People choose to live with humans. They are known as redcaps in Holland; nis in Scandinavia; brownies, hobgoblins or piskies in Britain; kobolds in Germany and domovoy in Russia. Their names differ, but their behaviour is similar. Each will work loyally for his household, for little reward, as long as no one upsets him.

BROWNIES AND HOBGOBLINS

Brownies and hobgoblins are small and raggedly dressed. They help with domestic jobs, usually at night. Brownies especially like to live on farms so they can work with animals. Piskies are similar, though more unreliable.

Payment is always the same – a bowl of best milk or cream and some freshly baked cake or bread, left for them to find. They are insulted if the offering is given to them directly. A gift of new clothes will send them away forever, possibly because it offends them or perhaps because they consider themselves paid off. Criticize or annoy them, and they will play spiteful tricks. In fact it is said that an angry brownie may even turn into a boggart (see page 23).

The terms hobgoblin and goblin have sometimes been used for the same beings, but usually it is agreed that hobgoblins are friendly while goblins are definitely not.

DOMOVOY

The domovoy looks like an old, grey-bearded man, wearing a grey robe or red shirt. He lives with a family, and if that family moves house he will go with them. They should put a slice of bread under the stove in the new house to welcome him in.

A domovoy's work should always be appreciated and he must only be referred to as Himself or Grandfather. He dislikes bad language. If really annoyed, he will burn the house down, but usually he will protect his chosen family and make himself useful.

The domovoy lives behind the stove and, like the redcap, is good at lighting hearth fires. Creaks and night noises are the sounds of the domovoy finishing off the household chores.

Kobolds will sweep the floor, wash dishes, and discover the secret places where the hens have laid their eggs.

ORIGINS OF LITTLE PEOPLE

These helpful beings do not all live in houses. Some prefer barns or outhouses, caves or the hollow hearts of huge trees. This fits in with a theory that all elvish folk are members of an early race of people, driven from their lands by newcomers. This would explain their need to be respected even though they must rely on the stronger race for food.

Another theory says these Little People are the spirits of dead ancestors. Many, though, choose to believe they are quite separate from humanity and are truly supernatural beings, dressed in brown or green, often with red caps, always with magical powers.

HOUSEHOLD HELPERS IN BOOKS AND FILMS

📖 *The Elves and the Shoemaker*
The Brothers Grimm

📖 *The Field Guide (The Spiderwick Chronicles)*
Tony DiTerlizzi and Holly Black

🎬 *Harry Potter and the Chamber of Secrets* (2002)

Harmful Little People

Goblins, boggarts, bogeymen and their kind are always hostile to humans, and so are imps, who are minor demons. At best they tease and frighten, at worst they do actual harm. It is unwise to speak of them and only a very foolish person would seek them out.

Surprisingly, goblins are fond of children. A goblin may even give a well-behaved child a present, although he will take delight in punishing a naughty child.

GOBLINS

Goblins are often invisible, but if seen are small, ugly and unpleasant-looking. They will pinch, punch and nip, frighten animals and terrify people. They sometimes live in houses, stables and barns, but often they live outside, usually near a pool, millpond or stream. The Erl King is a particularly dangerous goblin from the Black Forest in Germany who lures travellers to their death.

DREADFUL DANCERS

Northern France has the White Ladies, sometimes known as fées, who wait near bridges after dark until a lone man passes by. The White Lady will ask him to dance with her. If he accepts, she will release him at the end of the dance and he will be safe. If he refuses, she will throw him over the bridge or set her pet owls and cats on him.

Goblins have never been known to be helpful, but the Tokoloshi of South Africa does useful work around the house. However, he is dangerous because he works for a witch or sorcerer who will send him to torment or attack his victims. However, he will not harm a child, even if he is ordered to do so.

It is possible to keep these Little People at bay. A horseshoe hung over a door will prevent them from entering. A four-leafed clover does not only grant wishes, it also protects its owner from goblin-attack.

BOGGART AND BOGEYMAN

The boggart enjoys scaring people. Outside he may follow them in lonely places after dark; inside he will behave like a noisy poltergeist (see pages 130–131). The bogeyman has many names, including Boggelman in Germany, Bubak in Bohemia and Bocan in Ireland. He is a malicious goblin, covered in black hair, who can be dangerous but is more often just spiteful. Fortunately, these creatures are not very intelligent and can often be outwitted.

HARMFUL LITTLE PEOPLE IN BOOKS AND FILMS

📖 *The Boggart*
Susan Cooper

📖 *The Goblin Companion*
Brian Froud and Terry Jones

📖 *The Princess and the Goblin*
George MacDonald

🎥 *Labyrinth* (1986)

Underground

Dwarves live underground and look like small, elderly bearded men, with lined faces, gnarled hands and bright eyes. Just as elves are usually young, it seems dwarves are almost always old. Many of them are miners and skilled metal workers, and their underground homes are full of hand-crafted treasures and precious stones.

The bluecap appears in mines as a small blue flame. If treated with respect, bluecaps will lead miners to rich veins of ore or coal and forewarn them of danger, just as the knockers and wichtlein do.

THUMPERS AND LITTLE WIGHTS

In the old tin mines of Cornwall, the coal mines of Wales and throughout the working mines of northern Europe, dwarves are called thumpers or knockers because they communicate with humans by rapping and banging on the mine walls. Repeated knocking in one place means there is a rich seam there to be mined. Heavy digging and pounding noises warn of danger from flood or roof-fall. In Germany, where they are called wichtlein, or little wights, three distinct knocks foretell the death of a miner.

Dwarves are usually helpful and are believed to bring good fortune. However, it is wise to leave out food for them and never to swear or even whistle when they are around.

The household elves called kobolds (see page 21) also work in mines but there they are mischievous and likely to throw stones.

DWARVES IN BOOKS AND FILMS

📖 *Snow White and the Seven Dwarves*
The Brothers Grimm

📖 *Artemis Fowl: The Seventh Dwarf*
Eoin Colfer

📖 *The Hobbit*
J R R Tolkien

📖 *The Lord of the Rings*
J R R Tolkien

🎥 *Time Bandits* (1981)

BARBEGAZI

The barbegazi are dwarves who live in the Alps in France and Switzerland. Their name comes from the French *barbes glacées*, which means 'frozen beards'. Their white fur clothes, and the icicles in their hair and beards, make them very hard to see in winter. In summer they hibernate in caves and tunnels in the rock and do not come out until the first snowfall. Their greatest excitement is to surf on avalanches, although they will give low whistling cries to warn humans of the danger and will do their best to dig them out if they become trapped.

ULDRA

The dwarves who live within the Arctic Circle, in the far north of Norway, Sweden, Finland and Russia are called uldra. Like the barbegazi, they hibernate underground in summer. The uldra emerge on winter nights to care for the reindeer and moose who graze on the lichen and moss through the bleak months. They never leave their burrows in daylight because it dazzles them. Although the uldra are not unfriendly to humans, they will become enraged if reindeer herdsmen accidentally pitch their temporary tents over the narrow openings of their burrows.

Barbegazi have huge feet, which enable them to run across soft snow and ski down steep slopes.

25

Gremlins

Gremlins are the most recent of all known elfin-creatures. They were first noticed in *World War I (1914–18)* by the Royal Naval Air Service, UK, and later by Royal Air Force crews in India in the 1920s. These extremely mischievous creatures originally caused problems with aircraft engines.

NAMING GREMLINS

The name 'gremlins' is thought to be a blend of *Grimm's Fairy Tales* and Fremlins, the only beer then available to airmen.

There are several different descriptions of gremlins, though all agree that they have no wings but love flying, which is why they hitch rides on planes. Some say they look like a 50cm-tall rabbit with a sour expression; others that they are 30cm-tall elves with red jackets and green trousers; and several say they are 5cm-tall, with horns, webbed feet and leather flying jackets.

Author Roald Dahl (1916–90), who joined the British Royal Air Force at the start of World War II, chose them as the subject of his first novel, *The Gremlins*, published in 1943.

GREMLINS IN BOOKS

☐ *Electric Girl*
Michael Brennan

☐ *Troll Fell*
Katherine Langrish

☐ *The Greedy Gremlin*
Tracey West

☐ Sadly, Roald Dahl's novel
The Gremlins is out of print and
so cannot be bought in bookshops.

Grimm's Fairy Tales *is
a collection of folk and
fairy stories gathered
together by two German
brothers, Jacob Grimm
(1785–1863) and Wilhelm
Grimm (1786–1859),
early in the 19th century.*

GREMLIN BEHAVIOUR

The World War I gremlins lived in burrows at
the edges of airfields. Once on a plane, they
were able to cause any one of the controls to
malfunction or fail entirely. They would also
interfere with the wireless (radio) and drink
the fuel. The really powerful ones could
rearrange the stars in the sky to mislead the
navigator. Ground-based gremlins could cause
an entire airfield to rise or sink just as
a plane was coming in to land.

Nowadays, gremlins have managed to
creep into almost everything mechanical or
electronic. They can be blamed for countless
problems, from cars refusing to start to
computers behaving strangely or crashing.

*There is no record of a
gremlin actually flying any
kind of plane, but it seems
likely (because of their
fascination with planes)
that this was their
ultimate ambition.*

2

Elementals and nature spirits

Elementals are the spirits of the individual elements that combine to make up all things. Nature spirits — genius loci in *Latin* — are the spirits or guardians of specific places. Every glade, stream and pool, and every mountain, forest and tree has its own spirit, which is both its life-force and its protector.

Elementals

Everything is made up of a mixture of elements, in different amounts. In ancient Chinese and Eastern teachings, there are five elements — earth, fire, metal, water and wood — each with its symbolic creature or elemental. Earth is represented by a yellow phoenix; fire by a red pheasant; metal by a white tiger; water by a black turtle, sometimes combined with a serpent; wood by a green dragon.

THE FOUR ELEMENTALS

It is thought that a Sicilian philosopher called Empedocles (c.490–430BCE) first developed the idea of only four elements: earth, air, fire and water. Certainly Plato (c.428–348BCE) and Aristotle (385–322BCE) accepted it as a scientific fact. The belief that everything was made up of just four ingredients convinced some alchemists that it would be possible to change one into another — and many of them attempted to transform ordinary metal into gold.

EARTH ELEMENTALS

Gnomes belong to the earth. Earth is where they live and into earth is where they vanish. They are ancient and dark, and often dressed in a monk's habit. Usually hunched and small, they can shape-shift into giants at will.

Gnomes are not at all like garden gnomes, who are really dwarves, a mistake that began in early fairy tales.

FIRE ELEMENTALS

Salamanders are symbols for fire. Some believed their skin was so cold it could put fire out; others that they chose to live in flames and could even strengthen them. However, these were the Salamanders of fantasy. In reality, there are several kinds of these amphibious lizards and none of them, not even the black and gold European Fire Salamander, can survive flames.

ELEMENTALS IN BOOKS AND FILMS

📖 *The Tears of the Salamander*
Peter Dickinson

📖 *The Ragwitch*
Garth Nix

🎥 *Fantasia* (1940)

AIR ELEMENTALS

Sylphs are the light, ethereal spirits of the air. Like the gnomes and the undines, they were first named by Paracelcus (CE1493–1541), a physician and alchemist, whose real name was Theophrastus Bombastus von Hohenheim. He named himself 'Paracelcus', which meant 'greater than Celcus', a famous Roman authority on medicine.

WATER ELEMENTALS

Undines, or Nereids, are water elementals. They are rarely seen, though may sometimes become visible drifting in the spray from waterfalls or the mist that rises from the surface of water at dawn or dusk.

31

Nymphs

Nymphs are nature spirits who take the form of young and beautiful women. They are known in many different countries and cultures. There are several main groups — Oceanides of the ocean; Nereids of the sea; Naiads of springs, streams and rivers; Oreads of the mountains; Dryads of woods and forests; and Hamadryads of individual trees.

TREE NYMPHS

The Dryads are daughters of Zeus, the greatest of the Greek gods. They are not immortal, but they can live for many, many years — as long as the forest or wood they inhabit. They are especially fond of oak trees and often wear oak-leaf garlands. Although they are gentle, and usually have no quarrel with humans, they will do their best to protect their trees.

If a wood or forest is threatened, the Dryads will join together and use all their power to make it a frightening place for those who plan to cut it down. They are rarely seen, though humans who are still and quiet may glimpse them moving among their trees.

The Hamadryads do not move, each one is always a part of her own tree, and she will live only as long as the tree itself.

WATER NYMPHS

There are believed to be 50 sea nymphs, known as Nereids, daughters of Nereus, the wise old man of the sea. They share their name with the water elementals. The sea they live in is the Mediterranean and, unlike the Sirens (see pages 72–73), they are helpful to those who sail across it.

The nymphs who live in the wide oceans are called Oceanides, while the Naiads are the spirits of running water, from springs and streams to great rivers.

(see pages 72–73)

NYMPHS IN BOOKS

📖 *Apollo & Daphne: Masterpieces of Greek Mythology*
Antonia Barber (Narrator)

📖 *The Chronicles of Narnia*
C S Lewis

ARTEMIS

All the nymphs, in company with the mountain Oreads, the tree nymphs and the rest, follow the Greek goddess Artemis, who is called Diana in Roman mythology. She is a moon goddess and a mother goddess, associated with the countryside and with tree worship. She is a huntress, but she is also the protector of women as they give birth, of children and of all young animals.

THE STORY OF DAPHNE

Many of the nymphs have their own stories, and the Greek tale of Daphne is one of the best known. She was the daughter of a river god called Peneus and was, like all nymphs, beautiful. The sun god Apollo fell in love with her, but Daphne did not love him and she ran away. He chased her and caught her, but she called out for help to Mother Earth, Gaea, who protected Daphne by turning her into a laurel tree, of the kind also called the bay tree. Apollo sadly picked some of the leaves and made himself a crown. Then he promised that the tree should always be evergreen and never wither. In Greece, the laurel, or bay, is still called Daphne.

Forest and woodland spirits

orests and woodlands are full of spirits. Deep amongst the trees, where the light is dim and the forest sounds are strange, it is easy to sense their presence. Trees have long been regarded as sacred. The pillared aisles of old churches are like avenues of tall trees. In ancient Egypt, the sycamore was sacred; in ancient Rome it was the fig tree, called the bo tree in India; in Scandinavia it is the ash, and in the rest of Europe it is the mighty oak.

Every tree can be said to have its roots in the earth, the underworld; its trunk and fruits in the world of humans where people can reach them; and its branches stretching up to heaven, carrying the stars.

SATYRS AND FAUNS

The woods are the chosen home of many of the elves and fairies and also of some of the nymphs, especially the Dryads and Hamadryads (see pages 32–33). Nymphs are always female, but satyrs and fauns are always male. Called satyrs in Greek mythology and fauns in Roman mythology, they are the lazy, pleasure-loving followers of Pan. Some say they are the brothers of the nymphs. Others believe they are the sons of nymphs and goats, which is why they are human down to the waist, apart from their pointed ears and small horns, but have hairy goats' legs and cloven goat hooves.

Satyrs and fauns are wood-geniis, who love music and dancing, and are usually harmless to humans. Their favourite occupation is chasing nymphs.

MISCHIEVOUS LESHIES

The Russian leshies have wild green hair, long green beards and green eyes. Their blood is blue so their skin has a blue tone. In winter, they hibernate, but in spring they are at their most lively and mischievous. They will let out cries and whistles to confuse travellers and hunters and will lead them around in circles. To escape the spell, humans must take off their clothes and replace them back to front, and swap their shoes onto the wrong feet.

FINNISH FOREST SPIRITS

The Finnish forest spirits are friendly unless annoyed or mistreated. They will lead lost travellers to safety and help hunters to find game. When a hunter kills his prey, he must let some of the blood run onto the ground as a gift to the spirit, in gratitude for his help.

Leshies are shape-shifters who can be as tall as trees in the centre of the forest or as tiny as blades of grass at its edge. They throw no shadows.

FOREST AND WOODLAND SPIRITS IN BOOKS AND FILMS

📖 *Redwall* series
Brian Jacques

📖 *The Lion, the Witch and the Wardrobe*
C S Lewis

📖 *Hexwood*
Diana Wynne Jones

🎥 *FernGully:*
The Last Rainforest (1992)

🎥 *The Wizard of Oz* (1939)

Solitary forest spirits

The solitary forest spirits are among the most vigorous and powerful of them all. The dreaded Bokwus ranges over much of North America. The Green Man, a nature spirit known by many names, can be found throughout northern and eastern Europe. The territory of Herne the Hunter is small, Windsor Great Park in England, but he is no less terrible for that.

Pan likes to appear suddenly, frightening nymphs and humans alike. His name is the origin of the word 'panic'.

PAN

Pan is the son of Hermes, messenger of the Greek gods. He looks like a satyr, with his goats' legs and hooves, his horns and his beard, but he is not of their kind. He may seem to be part of a group of nymphs and fauns, dancing to the music of his pipes, but really he stands alone – there is only one Pan. He is a rural god, found in fields and pastures and woodland glades, caring for shepherds and their flocks and guiding hunters to their prey.

The cult of the horned god Cernunnos was widespread when the Celtic religion flourished in northern Europe. He may still visit a long-lost shrine among the oaks of Windsor Great Park.

HERNE THE HUNTER

Near the site of a fallen oak, which once grew in ancient forest-land at Windsor, in England, the unwary have caught sight of a terrifying figure. He rides a great black horse, followed by a pack of phantom hounds, and stag's antlers grow from his head. He is Herne the Hunter, who some say is a Celtic god of the underworld.

Others believe he was once human, a favourite of a king, until rival hunters persuaded the king to send him away. Herne hanged himself from the oak and now haunts the park when the country is in danger.

THE BOKWUS

Native Americans tell stories of the Bokwus, the dangerous spirit of the spruce forests. Anyone walking alone through the trees can sense the Bokwus watching, and may glimpse his war-painted face through the leaves. He lurks near the rivers that flow through the forest and, if he can, drowns fishermen and travellers so that he can steal their souls.

SOLITARY FOREST SPIRITS IN BOOKS AND FILMS

- *The Dark is Rising*
  Susan Cooper

- *A Wizard Abroad*
  Diane Duane

- *The Moon of Gomrath*
  Alan Garner

- *The Box of Delights*
  John Masefield

- *Robin of Sherwood —
  Series 1* (1983)

No matter how often he is cut down, the Green Man will always live again.

THE GREEN MAN

The Green Man is a mysterious and powerful spirit. No one knows how ancient he is. He is certainly pre-Christian — yet there are carvings of his leafy head in many Christian churches. He is the life-force of the plant kingdom, found all over Europe — sometimes with other names, The Old Man of the Woods, Jack-in-the-Green or The Leaf King. He dies in winter but is reborn each spring. Long ago, it was believed that human sacrifice was necessary to ensure his survival. Even today, there are towns in Europe where his effigy is carried in May Day processions.

Dangerous water spirits

Deep, dark pools are dangerous, and so are rapidly flowing rivers and wide lakes with unexpected currents. These treacherous inland waters tend to have vengeful spirits that are quite unlike the gentle nymphs and water elementals. The best way to avoid them is to keep well away from the edge.

AHUITZOTL

This vicious creature was the emblem of Ahuitzotl, emperor of the Aztecs from CE1486 to 1502, and it still bears his name. It is part-dog, part-monkey and has a long tail with a monkey-hand on the end. It hides in deep water, whimpering to encourage passing humans to come closer. Then it lashes out with its tail, grabs an ankle with its extra hand and drags its victim underwater to be drowned and then eaten.

This picture of the water spirit Ahuitzotl, lying in wait in a lake, is carved on a stone box that once held the ashes of Emperor Ahuitzotl.

WATER PEOPLE

Among the Slavonic peoples of central and eastern Europe, a drowned girl becomes a russalka, whose sole aim is to drown others. The German nixes are different – they do no harm and sometimes marry humans. They never cause drowning, but may dance on the surface of the water if someone is going to drown soon.

The vodyanoi is an eastern European water demon that lurks in millponds, lakes and streams, waiting to drown humans and animals.

THE BUNYIP

The Australian bunyip haunts rivers, lakes, creeks, swamps and billabongs. Its name means 'devil' in the Aboriginal language. It is reported to be a large and ferocious eater of humans, and its bellowing roar can terrify mortals for miles around. It seems to live on the border between reality and fantasy. Many so-called bunyips are probably leopard seals, which are certainly large and noisy. The rest, including those that capture and eat humans, are hostile water spirits, like Ahuitzotl.

DANGEROUS WATER SPIRITS IN BOOKS

☐ *The Kelpie's Pearls*
Molly Hunter

☐ *Silver Moon*
Ian Krykorka

📖 *The Bunyip of Berkeley's Creek*
Jenny Wagner

The water horse can mate with a normal horse. If a foal is born, it will not have magical powers. However, if asked to cross a ford, the foal will always lie down in the water.

WATER HORSES

The kelpie of Scotland, the ninnir of Iceland and the Scandinavian neck are shape-shifters (see page 107) that frequently appear in the form of horses. It is wise to keep well away from them. If a human climbs on the back of a water horse, it is likely to plunge into the deepest lake and drown its rider. However, if a human gains control of its bridle, the horse can be put to work in the fields. It has the strength of ten land horses, but does not like to be enslaved and will try every trick to escape.

Dangers by the wayside

In the days before travellers were protected within cars, trains and aeroplanes, every journey was dangerous and frightening. The roads were narrow, twisted and unlit, and most people travelled on foot, carrying a flickering lantern to show the way through the night. That was when the stories began — of wandering spirits and phantom lights, of faery dogs and deadly danger at crossroads.

THE POOKA

Leading travellers astray is just one of the pastimes of the Little People, but there are some creatures who do nothing else.

The pooka, who may be Robin Goodfellow in disguise (see page 18), is a shaggy horse. He invites the unwary to ride him, then tips his riders into a lonely bog. However, the pooka is mischievous rather than dangerous.

CROSSROADS

Crossroads are frightening places in many cultures. Some say that any crossing of the ways confuses the flow of earth's energy, creating a psychic whirlpool in which ghosts and spirits may become trapped. Traditionally, executed criminals and witches were taken there for burial — perhaps to make it difficult for their ghosts to find their way back. The queen of the ghosts, the Greek moon goddess Hecate, is the guardian of crossroads, especially those where three ways meet.

Faery dogs are hunters, about the size of a calf and usually green. The first and second time a faery dog barks it is a warning to flee, but the traveller who hears the third bark is doomed.

PHANTOM LIGHTS

Flickering lights moving across marshy land
sometimes look like slim, elfin figures, or
like a lantern carried by an invisible hand.
Any who follow risk being led into swamps,
and abandoned when the light vanishes as
suddenly as it appeared. In reality, it is
probably methane gas, given off by rotting
vegetation, which catches light and burns
with a pale flame. Alone in the dark, though,
it is easier to believe in a mischievous
Will O' The Wisp or Jack O'Lantern,
or in evil spirits and even messengers
of death (see pages 124–125).

Phantom lights have other names, including
foxfire, *ignis fatuus* (which is Latin for 'foolish
fire') and corpse-light when the lights are
seen hovering above a graveyard.

*A traveller who trusts a phantom light carried by a goblin or
other fairy being is likely to be led into a marsh to drown.*

DANGERS BY THE WAYSIDE IN BOOKS AND FILMS

📖 *The Ghost in the Noonday Sun*
Sid Fleischman

📖 *Jack O'Lantern: A Halloween Tale*
Eric Martone

🎬 *The Nightmare Before Christmas* (1993)

DESERT SPIRITS

Under the surface of the Sahara desert there
is a strange world inhabited by a race of spirits
who rise into the world of humans to cause harm.
Their spinning dances create sandstorms, their
movements underground cause camels to trip
and fall. They will also drink wells dry before
thirsty travellers can reach them.

In lonely, rocky places in northern Australia,
the mimis live in narrow cracks and crevices.
They look almost human, but have such long, thin,
fragile bones they are afraid of the wind in case it
snaps them. They keep wallabies as pets and eat
yams – but they also eat people, so travellers are
advised to sing and shout to frighten them off.

The manticore — a savage creature with the
body of a lion, the face of a man, three rows
of teeth in each jaw, the speed of a deer and
a voice like a trumpet — was almost certainly
an exaggerated description of a tiger.

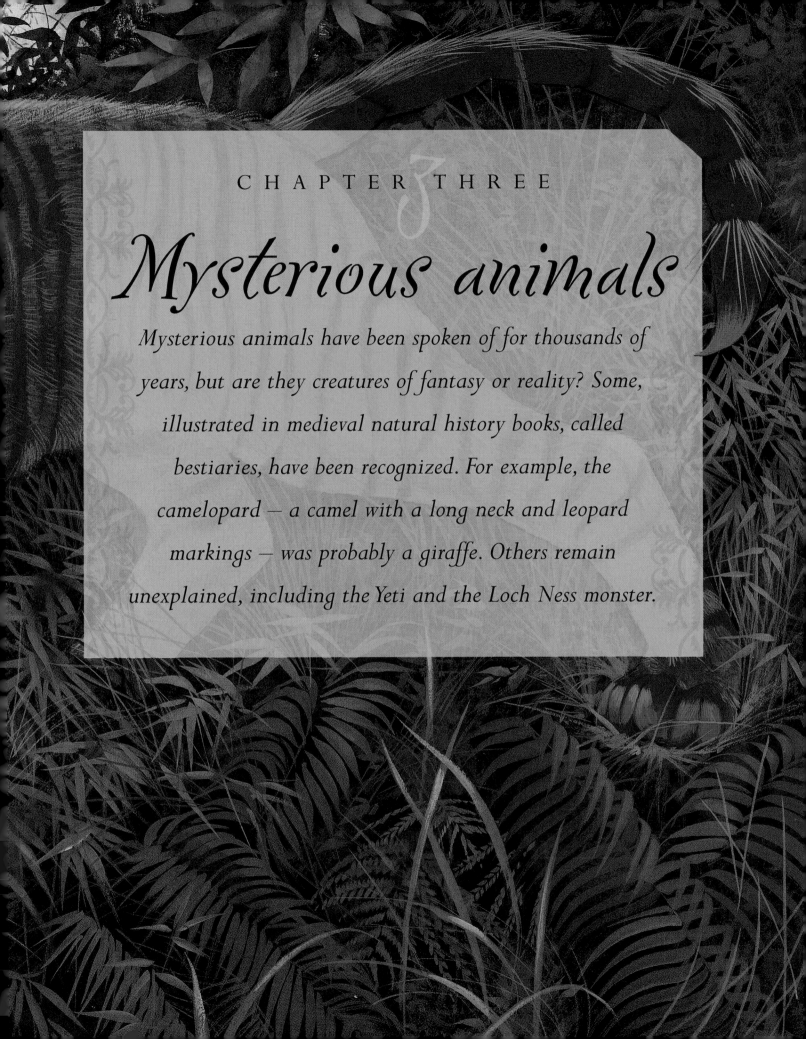

Mysterious animals

Mysterious animals have been spoken of for thousands of years, but are they creatures of fantasy or reality? Some, illustrated in medieval natural history books, called bestiaries, have been recognized. For example, the camelopard — a camel with a long neck and leopard markings — was probably a giraffe. Others remain unexplained, including the Yeti and the Loch Ness monster.

Ape-men of the mountains

Yeti is a Tibetan name that means 'magical creature'.

Tales of mysterious ape-like creatures living above the snowline in remote mountain regions have been told for centuries. In the Himalayas, their name is Yeti. In Sumatra, they are Orang Pendek. In North America, there is Sasquatch, or Bigfoot. Rarely photographed, never caught or killed, many believe these beasts to be imaginary — but as recently as 2003 an expedition set out for the Himalayas to find proof of their existence.

THE YETI

Sightings of the Yeti, sometimes called the Abominable Snowman, in the Himalayas have been reported by local people and mountaineers, explorers and scientists. Some have also heard a loud, yelping call that they can only explain as the Yeti's cry.

The first report to reach the West was in 1925 from a Greek photographer, N A Tombazi, who was in the Himalayas with a British geological expedition. He saw a man-like, hairy figure in the distance, pulling up shrubs, apparently searching for roots to eat.

Numerous treks have failed to find the Yeti, though several have found tracks that do not seem to have been made by any known animal.

This is one of several photographs of enormous footprints in the snow, but were they made by a Yeti? Animal tracks are known to change in shape and size as the snow around them melts.

44

SASQUATCH OR BIGFOOT

Sasquatch or Bigfoot is said to be like the Yeti, the height of an average man or taller, with a strong body and limbs, and dark red-brown hair. Its footprints are large and its stride is long.

If it seems strange that such a creature should be hard to find, it is worth remembering there are more than 388,485km^2 of wilderness in the American North West.

In Washington State, people still remember an experienced skier who disappeared on Mount St Helens 50 years ago. The mountain rescue team found his tracks, which showed he had made a rash and dangerous descent and then dropped down a steep canyon, where he vanished. Their only explanation was that he had been chased by something truly terrible.

Top right: A still from a 1967 documentary about Bigfoot (right), made in northern California. Many insist this was faked by a man in a monkey-suit. Others point out that the moving footage shows the action of huge muscles in the shoulders, back and thighs, which would only be visible on a real animal, not through a fur costume.

APE-MEN IN BOOKS AND FILMS

📖 *The Bigfoot Mystery: The Adventure Begins*
Robert Leiterman, Matt Moneymaker

📖 *Yeti Boy*
Kara May

🎥 *Bigfoot and the Hendersons* (1987)

🎥 *Monsters, Inc.* (2001)

In lakes

Tales of water monsters come from every country that has large, deep lakes within its borders. These great lakes are certainly big enough to hide a massive creature, and some are linked to the sea by underground caverns. Reports of sightings go back hundreds of years. Prehistoric rock drawings show animals very similar to plesiosaurs, and very like more recent descriptions of Nessie, Ogopogo and the rest.

This famous photograph of Nessie, the Loch Ness monster, was taken in 1934 by a London surgeon. In 1994, however, it emerged that the photograph was fake – the 'monster' in the picture is actually a toy submarine fitted with a plastic neck and head.

LAKE MONSTERS

The Loch Ness monster in Scotland and Ogopogo in Lake Okanogan, Canada, are the most famous, but there are many others. A mysterious beast has been reported in Lake Störsjon, Sweden, and a group of monsters was seen in China's Lake Tianchi as recently as 2003. Several have been given pet names – Issie lurks in Japan's Lake Ikada; Slimy Slim has been seen in Payette Lake, Idaho, USA. However, most people who have actually seen a lake monster have said they felt very frightened and over-awed.

NESSIE

The Loch Ness monster (nicknamed Nessie) from Loch Ness, Scotland, has been observed on dry land, but only briefly. Once spotted, it hurried back to the water, with a rocking motion like a seal on land. Descriptions suggest it was bigger than any seal, though, and its long neck suggested a plesiosaur, an aquatic dinosaur thought to be extinct.

There have been fewer sightings in recent years. Perhaps water pollution and human disturbance have prevented these creatures, whatever they are, from breeding.

OTHER EXPLANATIONS

Sightings of lake monsters may really be glimpses of something else. Deep waters, which are cold at the bottom and warmer at the top, have strong currents that create swirling movements. Floating clumps of rotting vegetation give off gases which can move them through the water on streams of bubbles. Otters or seals could be mistaken for something strange. Also, no lake monster has been caught, alive or dead, and searches using sonar and divers have found nothing.

However, visibility is bad in the depths, and there have been very many reliable witnesses over the years. Also, there are photographs — although some have been revealed to be fakes.

LAKE MONSTERS IN BOOKS AND FILMS

📖 *Nessie the Loch Ness Monster*
Richard Brassey

📖 *The Water Horse*
Dick King-Smith

📖 *Loch*
Paul Zindel

🎥 *Loch Ness* (1996)

🎥 *Scooby Doo and the Loch Ness Monster* (2004)

The name Ogopogo comes from a British comedy song of the 1920s. The native Canadians are more respectful — they use the name N'haitaka, which means water demon.

In the sea

For centuries, people who have sailed the oceans have brought back stories of giant sea serpents. Often, they were accused of exaggerating or imagining things. The same disbelief greeted stories of monster waves, up to 20m high. Recently, though, satellite photography has shown that there really are freak waves out there, some measuring as much as 30m. So, possibly, strange creatures do indeed swim in our oceans and seas.

TWO SIGHTINGS

In l966, John Ridgway and Chay Blyth rowed across the Atlantic Ocean, from the USA to Ireland, in an open boat. Early one morning, while Blyth slept, Ridgway saw 'a writing shape, two feet [60cm] wide and perhaps 40 feet [12m] long'. It swam straight towards the boat then dived and disappeared underneath it.

In 1977, the *Zuiyo Maru*, a Japanese boat fishing off New Zealand, pulled up a huge decomposing body in its trawl nets. It was too heavy and disgusting to keep on board. The crew photographed it, took tissue samples, measured it and threw it back. In all the years that have followed, no one has succeeded in identifying it.

SEA MONSTERS IN BOOKS AND FILMS

📖 *The Kraken*
Gary Crew

📖 *The Voyage of the Dawn Treader*
C S Lewis

📖 *O'Sullivan Stew*
Hudson Talbott

🎥 *20,000 Leagues Under the Sea*
(1954)

🎥 *Godzilla* (1998)

It has been suggested that Leviathan and Behemoth, the huge water monsters of the Old Testament in the Bible, are based on the whale and the hippopotamus. They are larger and more important than that, though, as they are not just mythical creatures, but also symbols of divine power.

THE KRAKEN

Most sightings of sea monsters describe serpentine necks and thrashing tails. The legendary kraken is different. Early descriptions claim it to be the size of a small island, with massive tentacles that it uses for swimming and for grasping fish. It is not usually aggressive, but it is still deadly dangerous. It is so large it creates a vast wave when it surfaces, and then drags the water into a powerful whirlpool when it submerges. Either of these threatens the survival of sailing vessels unlucky enough to be near. Fishermen, realizing the water has become unexpectedly shallow beneath their boat, head for shore at once knowing they have drifted above a hunting kraken that may rise at any time.

The kraken is now generally thought to be a giant squid, or giant cuttlefish. The giant squid may not be the size of an island, but it can measure a monstrous 12m long, with thrashing tentacles and saucer-like eyes.

The shield bearing the cross of St George shows that this knight is the saint himself, battling the ancient dragon (see page 54).

4

Fabulous beasts

Fabulous beasts were originally born from human imagination. They were created to explain human nature — love, cruelty, courage and fear — and also to account for natural events — storms, drought and floods. This blend of fiction and reality has given these beasts a freedom and power that sometimes allows them to cross the borders between fantasy and the real world.

Dragons in the East

Eastern dragons are weather-lords, bringers of rain, guardians of springs and rivers and lakes, and symbols of change. The Japanese dragon is more of a sea or river god. In China, the dragons sleep at the bottom of pools in the dry winter season. In the spring they rise up in the form of rain clouds. Storms are caused by dragons fighting in the air, floods by dragons fighting in the water. In the East the dragon is very powerful, but usually benevolent.

We know this dragon is a Chinese imperial dragon because he has five claws. Ordinary Chinese dragons and Korean dragons have four and Japanese dragons have only three. In ancient China, a person could be put to death for using the image of a five-toed dragon.

BORN FLYERS

Dragons lay eggs that do not hatch for 3,000 years. When their time comes, a hole appears in the shell and a tiny snake emerges. It grows into a full-sized dragon in minutes and flies up to the sky in a whirlwind. Unlike Western dragons, Chinese dragons do not have wings. They fly by their own energy.

Dragons are often shown holding, or chasing, a small globe which may be the moon, or the pearl of wisdom, or the egg that is the source of all life. This globe often has jagged, flame-like shapes coming out of it, which suggests it could also be a symbol of thunder and lightning.

EASTERN DRAGONS IN STORIES AND FILMS

📖 *Fire and Wings: Dragon Tales from East and West*
Marianne Carus and Nilesh Mistry

📖 *A Time of Golden Dragons*
Song Nan Zhang

📖 *The Dragon Prince*
Laurence Yep

🎥 *Spirited Away (2001)*

It was believed that no rain could fall until a dragon rose into the sky, so in times of drought every effort was made to encourage him wake up and fly. Better still was to disturb two dragons in the hope they would battle with each other until the storm clouds broke and watered the earth.

DRAGON LORE

The Yellow Dragon only emerges from his river when a holy man rules the country. It is said that when Fu Hsi, the first of the Ten Emperors, was on the throne, the Yellow Dragon rose from the water with the earliest Chinese characters marked on his back. In this way he gave the secret of writing to the emperor and so to his people.

In Vietnam, carved dragons on roofs are a protection against fire. Dragon-fire and earthly fire are opposites. Earthly fire is put out by water. Dragon-fire burns in water but is put out by earthly fire.

Dragons in the West

Western dragons are usually dangerous. Some are so evil they are said to be the devil himself. Like Eastern dragons they are associated with water, but are more likely to bring destructive floods than plant-nourishing showers. Unlike Eastern dragons, they are usually hunted and slain.

In the distant past, fossilized skulls of dinosaurs, or bones of large bears found in caves, were thought to be dragon remains. Throughout history there have been hoaxes — including this recent specially made 'baby dragon' preserved in a jar.

DRAGON SLAYERS

St Michael fought the devil-dragon and threw him out of heaven, but the most famous dragon slayer is St George. Legend tells that in his time (about 2,000 years ago) there was a terrible dragon who lived in a lake and demanded human sacrifices. St George chanced to pass just as the king's daughter had been tied up and left for the dragon to eat. In some tellings, he killed the dragon at once. In others he wounded it, and he and the princess tied it with her sash and led it to the heart of the kingdom to kill it in front of the people.

Dragons are sometimes slain for the hoard of treasure they guard. Most believe it is the gold and riches buried with long-dead kings, but some say it is the gold of the sun, which sets and then rises again, and that the treasure the dragon guards is immortality.

Traditionally, the Western dragon is killed by an iron lance. The first iron known to humans is likely to have been found in meteorites. Because meteorites fall to earth from the sky, it was believed that it had come from heaven and therefore had the power to destroy evil.

GOOD DRAGONS

However, not all Western dragons are bad. When Uther Pendragon (father of King Arthur) was born, two golden dragons appeared in the sky to herald the birth of a chieftain, and dragon images appeared on shields and battle standards. There are even stories of dragons kept as pets, and also of dragons who help humans, such as Falkor the Luck Dragon in *The Neverending Story*.

WESTERN DRAGONS IN BOOKS AND FILMS

📖 *Dr Ernest Drake's Dragonology*
Ernest Drake

📖 *Eragon*
Christopher Paolini

📖 *The Hobbit*
J R R Tolkien

🎬 *Dragonheart* (1996)

🎬 *The Neverending Story* (1984)

The unicorn

The unicorn, also known as Kirin in Japan and Ki Lin in China, is one of the most beautiful creatures of fantasy. It is usually seen as an elegant white horse with a long spiral horn on its forehead. The horn has healing powers. Also, it can detect poison in a well, in a watering hole or in any liquid, then purify it and make it safe.

Goblets made from unicorn horn were used by rulers who feared enemies might poison them. The horn was usually a tusk from a narwhal — a type of whale.

WESTERN UNICORNS

Western unicorns were first mentioned in 398BCE by Greek historian Ctesias who, when writing down travellers' tales, described them as 'wild asses which are as big as a horse, even bigger. Their bodies are white, their heads are purple and their eyes are deep blue. They have a single horn on their forehead which is approximately half-a-metre long.' He called this creature Monoceros, which translates as 'one horn'.

'The Lady and the Unicorn' is one of six famous large tapestries woven in Flanders, Belgium, in the late 15th century. Five of them illustrate the five senses: taste, smell, hearing, touch and sight. The meaning of this last one, however, remains mysterious.

EASTERN UNICORNS

The Ki Lin (or Ch'i Lin) described in the ancient texts of China are different from the Western unicorn, both in appearance and character. They are described as having the body of a deer and the hooves of a horse, with a fine head and single horn. They are so gentle they tread carefully for fear of harming insects.

In Japanese legend, the Kirin is a unicorn similar to Ki Lin, but its body is covered in scales.

Eastern unicorns are seen to be peaceful and bringers of good luck.

CAPTURING A UNICORN

Western unicorns are wild and aggressive creatures, and catching one is very difficult. Writings from the 12th century advised hunters how to catch a unicorn: the beast is enchanted by a young girl and falls asleep on her lap. This is when the hunters strike, capturing the sleeping unicorn and cutting off its horn. Wealthy nobles boasted that they had bought unicorn horns which they used to detect poison in their food and drink.

UNICORNS IN BOOKS AND FILMS

📖 *The Last Unicorn*
Peter Beagle

📖 *Spellhorn*
Berlie Doherty

📖 *The Little White Horse*
Elizabeth Goudge

🎥 *Legend* (1985)

Legend tells that wild unicorns can be tamed by young maidens.

Fantasy horses

For centuries, horses have been valued over most other animals. Symbols of power and wealth, horses have been tamed, trained, ridden, sacrificed, buried with kings and warriors, and used to pull peasant carts, royal coaches and chariots of war. At the same time, their speed, strength, beauty and grace have placed them in the sky with the gods. Mystical, magical horses appear in stories from almost every country on earth.

THE HORSES OF THE SUN

The sun is carried across the sky in a chariot, pulled by a single, powerful stallion or by a team of horses – so we are told by most of the mythologies of the ancient civilizations. In Norse mythology, there are two horses – Alsvid the Allswift and Arvak the Early Riser.

The golden chariot of the Greek sun god Helios is drawn by nine white, winged horses with fire flaring from their nostrils and the light of day pouring from their shining manes.

Many of the other gods travelled behind teams of celestial horses. Odin, the greatest of the Norse gods, is said to have ridden an eight-legged horse and, as night falls, the moon goddess Selene drives her own pale horse across the heavens.

Vertebrates (animals with backbones) have four limbs — either four legs, or two arms and two legs. Pegasus is one of those rare creatures who, like winged dragons, have six limbs — four legs and two wings.

Some say that Poseidon (also called Neptune), the god of the sea, created the first horses. To this day, people looking at a stormy sea refer to the wind-whipped crests of the waves as white horses.

PEGASUS

The gentle, winged horse Pegasus sprang from the blood of the terrible Gorgon Medusa after Perseus beheaded her. Pegasus flew to the home of the Muses on Mount Helicon and, to their delight, created the spring of inspiration, Hippocrene, by stamping his foot on the ground.

When the hero Bellerophon was given the task of killing the dreadful Chimera (see page 64), the Greek goddess Athene gave him a magical golden bridle with which to catch and tame Pegasus. This meant he could fly above the Chimera on the wonderful horse and rain arrows on her from a safe distance. Later, he became over-ambitious and tried to ride Pegasus to Mount Olympus, the home of the gods, where no mortal could go. The gods sent a gadfly to sting and startle Pegasus who threw Bellerophon back to earth. However, the immortal horse was welcomed into the heavenly stables and has now been set in the sky as a constellation.

FANTASY HORSES IN BOOKS AND FILMS

📖 *Stravaganza: City of Stars*
Mary Hoffman

📖 *The Magician's Nephew*
C S Lewis

📖 *Pegasus, the Flying Horse*
Jane Yolen

🎥 *Clash of the Titans* (1981)

🎥 *Hercules* (1997)

Fire and feather

Imagine a creature formed from the lion (King of the Beasts) and the eagle (King of the Birds), large enough to block out the sun and with the strength to lift a horse and its rider into the sky. Consider a bird that is truly unique, lays no eggs, but is reborn every thousand years out of its own ashes. Both of these creatures, and the offspring of one, are spoken of in the mountains of India and Arabia.

High in the Indian mountains, griffins dig gold to make their nests. They also collect the stones known as agate, which have medicinal properties and will protect their chicks from sickness. Humans who try to steal their gold are unlikely to survive, especially as griffins feed their young on human remains. However, adult griffin prefers to eat live horses.

THE PHOENIX

The Arabian phoenix is as rare as it is possible to be — there is only one in the world. When it knows it is dying, it builds itself a funeral pyre and sings a beautiful song while the sun sets it alight. Both pyre and bird are reduced to ashes. From these, a new phoenix arises. Traditionally, it collects the ashes of its former self and flies, surrounded by other birds, to Heliopolis, the ancient Egyptian City of the Sun. There it delivers the ashes to the priests and flies back to its home in Arabia.

The Feng-Hwang, known as the Chinese phoenix, and the Ho-o, the Japanese phoenix, are rather different. Instead of a solitary bird, there is a pair, and their lovely songs are omens of peace and joy.

THE GRIFFIN

Whether its name is spelt griffin or gryphon, this is a majestic beast. It has the body and legs of a lion and the head, wings and beak of an eagle. Sometimes it has a serpent's tail. Its back is feathered and its lion's feet are armed with eagle's claws. These claws are prized because, although they cannot purify poison like the unicorn's horn, they can warn of its presence by changing colour.

The phoenix is as large as an eagle and its plumage is dazzlingly beautiful — red, gold, blue and purple.

THE HIPPOGRIFF

This beast is born when a horse mates with a griffin — something that could never happen because griffins hate horses and eat them when they can. The Roman poet Virgil, who lived between 70 and 19BCE, referred to crossing griffins with horses as an example of impossibility, and later, early in the 16th century, Ludovico Ariosto created the impossible hippogriff in his epic poem *Orlando Furioso*.

> ### GRIFFINS AND PHOENIXES IN BOOKS AND FILMS
>
> 📖 ***The Wrath of Mulgarath***
> Tony DiTerlizzi and Holly Black
>
> 📖 ***The Phoenix and the Carpet***
> E Nesbit
>
> 📖 ***The Year of the Griffin***
> Diana Wynne Jones
>
> 🎥 ***Harry Potter and the Chamber of Secrets*** (2002)

Giant birds

Giant birds fly through the folk tales, mythology and fantasy of most countries. The three best known are probably the Garuda Bird, the Roc and the Thunderbird. Giant birds are usually deadly enemies of snakes — except in Central America where the god-king, Quetzalcoatl, is both bird and serpent. His name made up of Quetzal, a rare Guatemalan bird, and coatl meaning 'snake'. He is a wind god, the morning and evening star, and the wise ruler who discovered the food, maize.

The very ancient and holy Garuda Bird is sometimes the chosen steed of the Indian god, Vishnu.

THE GARUDA BIRD

The Indian Garuda Bird is often shown as part-bird and part-man, although originally he was an eagle. The Garuda Bird is a demon is Buddhist mythology. In Hindu tales, he is the bird of life and carrier of knowledge, at the same time a creator and a destroyer. In Indonesian mythology, he preys on humans. The Garuda Bird is the enemy of snakes and of the Nagas (see page 67). Even dragons fear him, and his image can scare an Eastern dragon into rising from his pool and bringing rain.

*The coc...
so muc...
will re...*

THE ROC

The Roc, or Rukh, (left) is a bird so strong it can lift an elephant as easily as a hawk lifts a mouse. Its wingspan is 15m, its egg towers higher than a man, and its claws can be made into drinking goblets. Some medieval collectors boasted of owning one of its feathers, but this was probably a frond from the huge raffia palm, also known as the feather palm.

Some descriptions of the Roc may be exaggerated accounts of real birds, such as the condor of South America. Or they may have been inspired by the sight of an egg from the elephant bird of Madagascar, which became extinct in the 16th century. It was unable to fly, but its egg was enormous.

The Thunderbird is a spirit, the symbol of the electrical energy of the storm, which can bring terrible devastation or essential nurturing rain.

GIANT BIRDS IN BOOKS AND FILMS

📖 *One Thousand and One Arabian Nights*
Geraldine McCaughrean

📖 *Mythical Birds and Beasts from Many Lands*
Margaret Mayo and Jane Ray

📖 *How the Music Came to the World*
Hal Ober

🎥 *The Seventh Voyage of Sinbad* (1958)

THUNDERBIRD

Throughout native North American legend, the Thunderbird represents the storm. His wings make the sound of thunder, his eyes send out lightning flashes, and he brings rain. He is seen in visions rather than in reality because in reality he is surrounded and hidden by dense clouds. The Thunderbird may be dangerous, carrying off animals and people, or he may be benevolent, granting good fortune.

Guardians of worlds and doors

Entrances to other worlds are powerful places and their guardians are impressive and sometimes terrifying. They are not always animals. The Norse god Heimdall guards the rainbow bridge between earth and the world of the Scandinavian gods. The Roman god Janus guards doorways and is two-headed so he can keep watch both ways. However, it is the guardian beasts that are the most dramatic — especially the great mythic dogs of the underworld.

CERBERUS

The hound of Hades, the Greek god of death, is Cerberus. He is the guardian of the underworld, born from the same parents as the Chimera (see page 64). He has three heads, terrible jaws that drip venom, the tail of a dragon and, sometimes, serpents growing out of his back. He greets the newly dead at the entrance to the underworld, allowing them in, but never allowing them out again.

Cerberus can be calmed with honey cakes, though it is essential to take one for each head. Orpheus soothed him by playing the lyre when he tried to rescue his wife, Eurydice, from the realms of the dead.

The twelfth labour of Heracles was to kidnap him. Hades permitted this so long as the dog was returned unharmed. Heracles used his great strength to drag the wildly barking hound briefly into the upper world — and wherever Cerberus' saliva fell, there grew poisonous plants called aconites, also named monkshood or wolf's bane.

Cerberus is the huge and terrible guardian dog of the underworld. His name comes from the Greek kerberos, *meaning 'demon of the pit.'*

GUARDIAN BEASTS IN BOOKS AND FILMS

📖 *Prince Orpheus*
Paule du Bouchet

📖 *Tales of the Norse Gods*
Barbara Leonie Picard

📖 *Twelve Labours of Hercules*
James Riordan

🎥 *Harry Potter and the Philosopher's Stone* (2001)

Janus, the Roman god of gates, doors and passageways, is also the god of new beginnings. The month of January is named after him.

GARM AND THE DOGS OF YAMA

In Norse mythology, Hel is the goddess of Helheim, the Land of the Dead, and Garm is her hound, guardian of death's gate. He is an enormous creature with four eyes. His body is usually covered in the blood of the slain.

In Indian teachings, Yama was the first being to die, and so he reigns in the next world and guides those who must journey to it. His kingdom is not the dark underworld but the bright outer sky. Yama's four-eyed hounds – Syama the black and Sabala the spotted – are as fierce as Cerberus or Garm, but they are also helpful. They are often sent out to find the dead and lead them safely to Yama's kingdom of light. Even so, the dead are given raw meat for their journey to pacify the hounds.

There are nine Muses. They are
generally agreed to be Clio for history; Calliope
for epic poetry; Erato for love poetry; Euterpe for lyric
poetry; Thalia for comedy; Melpomene for tragedy; Terpsichore
for dance; Polyhymnia for hymns and Urania for astronomy.

CHAPTER FIVE

Mythical beings

Some mythical beings, such as Sirens, centaurs and Cyclops, are the creations of classical mythology. Others, such as mermaids and giants, owe their existence partly to travellers' tales. However, they have all found their way, in one form or another, into the world of fantasy. In any case, it could be said that all ideas, including fantastical ones, come from those early Greek mythical beings, the classical Muses, the goddesses of inspiration.

Beautiful but dangerous

In ancient Greece and Rome, boats were propelled by oarsmen, whose work was especially hard if currents and tides were against them. Without maps or charts, they relied on the words of others to guide them. Without instruments of navigation, they kept close to land, risking shallows and hidden rocks. Sea travel was perilous, and the ever-present dangers were given many names, such as Scylla, Charybdis and the legendary Sirens.

The hero Odysseus, or Ulysses, was saved from the Sirens by the enchantress Circe. On her advice, he ordered his men to melt wax to block their ears. Then Odysseus asked to be tied to the ship's mast so he could hear the Sirens' songs but would not be able to change the direction of the ship, however persuasive they were.

THE SIRENS

The Sirens had the bodies and feet of birds, but the faces and upper parts of beautiful women. They lived on a small, barren island off southern Italy, and were famous for the loveliness of their singing voices, and for their songs, which offered knowledge of the past and the future to all who heard them. Despite this, they were deadly. Mariners, lured to the island by their singing, found the Sirens surrounded by the bones and corpses of their earlier victims and knew they were trapped.

Later, Jason and the Argonauts sailed by in their quest for the Golden Fleece. Orpheus, son of the god Apollo, was with them, and he played the lyre and sang even more beautifully than the Sirens. His songs overcame them, and the Sirens were turned into rocks for all eternity.

SCYLLA AND CHARYBDIS

Scylla was once a water nymph, and there are many different stories of how she became a monster. In all of them, though, it was a jealous goddess or enchantress who changed her into a writhing, serpent-like form with six heads and a voice like the howling of dogs. She lived in a cave, probably in the Straits of Medina between Italy and Sicily, and sent out her heads on their long, snake-like necks to snatch sailors from their ships and devour them.

Opposite her, on the other side of the narrow straits, was Charybdis, a powerful whirlpool (left) strong enough to swallow the largest vessel. Navigating between these two terrors was, literally, a matter of life and death.

SIRENS, CHARYBDIS AND SCYLLA IN BOOKS AND FILMS

📖 *The Adventures of Ulysses*
Bernard Evslin

📖 *The Odyssey*
Robin Lister

📖 *Jason and the Argonauts*
John Malam

📖 *Sirens and Sea Monsters*
Mary Pope Osborne

🎥 *Sinbad: Legend of the Seven Seas*
(2003)

73

Hideous and dangerous

The Furies, the Gorgons and the Harpies are among the most ferocious and hideous characters in Greek mythology. The Furies can, on rare occasions, deliver good fortune, but most of the time they, like the others, bring terror.

THE GORGONS

The three Gorgons, known as The Grim Ones, are Euryale the Wanderer, Sthenno the Strong One and Medusa the Ruler. Sometimes they have the heads of women, sometimes of dogs or lions, and sometimes they have tusks like a wild boar. One glance from a Gorgon can turn a person to stone. Two of the dreaded sisters are immortal, but Medusa was mortal and Perseus succeeded in killing her by using her reflection in his shield to guide his hand, and then cutting off her head. When drops of her blood fell into the sea, they became scarlet coral branches, still known as Gorgonia.

THE FURIES

It is never wise to speak the name of The Furies, call them instead The Kindly Ones to calm them. There are three – Alecto the Endless, Tisiphone the Punisher, and Megaera the Jealous Rager. They are fearsome crones with the heads of dogs and hair made of snakes. They carry torches to hunt down wrongdoers and whips with metal studs to deliver vicious beatings.

The Furies are avengers – avenging any who have been harmed by lies or, worse, murdered by their children.

THE HARPIES

No one knows how many Harpies there are, but they are called The Seizers or The Snatchers because they carry away human beings or steal their food. Some say they were once beautiful, and certainly they have the faces and breasts of women, but they have the bodies and wings of vultures, and terrible long claws. They are among the most dangerous creatures of the underworld, appearing in storms and whirlwinds, and leaving behind a foul and putrid stench.

The only thing that frightens Harpies away is the sound made by a brazen (brass) instrument.

All the Gorgons, including Medusa, the best-known, have writhing serpents in place of hair.

GORGONS, FURIES AND HARPIES IN BOOKS AND FILMS

📖 *The Odyssey*
Homer

📖 *Perseus*
Geraldine McCaughrean

🎥 *Clash of the Titans* (1981)

🎥 *The Seventh Voyage of Sinbad* (1958)

75

Part-man, part-beast

In fantasy and mythology there live many strange life-forms, made up of parts of more familiar animals, usually as a result of the unexpected pairings of their parents. Some, like the lion-goat-serpent Chimera are terrifying; others, such as the maiden-fish mermaids, are beautiful. The most famous of the land-based composite creatures are the centaurs — part-man, part-horse; the satyrs and fauns — part-man, part-goat; and the bull-headed man known as the Minotaur.

CHIRON

The best of the centaurs was the wise and gentle Chiron, who was taught the healing arts by the gods. He became a teacher, and great heroes and the sons of gods were brought to him for tutoring. One of these was Aesculapius, or Asclapios, son of the god Apollo and a mortal girl. Chiron taught him so well that Aesculapius soon overtook him in learning, and became the founder and god of medicine. When the immortal Chiron was accidentally wounded with a poisoned arrow, he gave away his immortality rather than live in pain forever. In memory of him, Zeus, the ruler of the Greek gods, placed Chiron's image in the night sky as the constellation of Sagittarius.

Most centaurs are wild and aggressive. Some stories say they were once giants, Titans, who fought the early gods, were defeated and given the bodies of horses as a punishment. Other tales say that they came from the union of a giant with a race of horses. It may even be that early Greeks, encountering invading warriors on horseback, assumed man and beast were one creature.

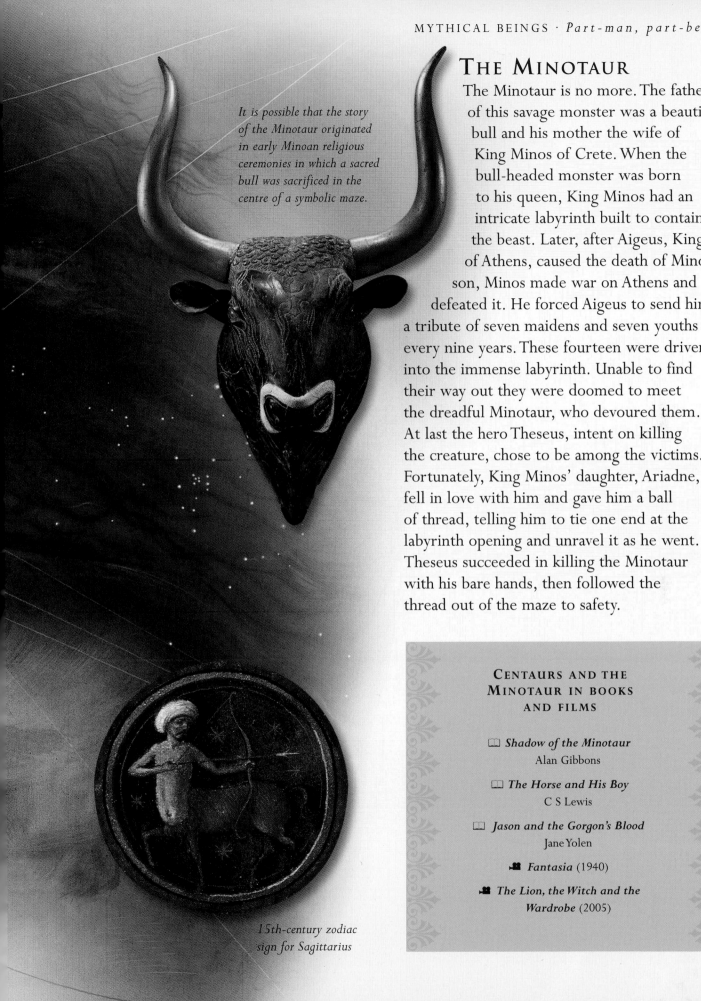

It is possible that the story of the Minotaur originated in early Minoan religious ceremonies in which a sacred bull was sacrificed in the centre of a symbolic maze.

THE MINOTAUR

The Minotaur is no more. The father of this savage monster was a beautiful bull and his mother the wife of King Minos of Crete. When the bull-headed monster was born to his queen, King Minos had an intricate labyrinth built to contain the beast. Later, after Aigeus, King of Athens, caused the death of Minos' son, Minos made war on Athens and defeated it. He forced Aigeus to send him a tribute of seven maidens and seven youths every nine years. These fourteen were driven into the immense labyrinth. Unable to find their way out they were doomed to meet the dreadful Minotaur, who devoured them. At last the hero Theseus, intent on killing the creature, chose to be among the victims. Fortunately, King Minos' daughter, Ariadne, fell in love with him and gave him a ball of thread, telling him to tie one end at the labyrinth opening and unravel it as he went. Theseus succeeded in killing the Minotaur with his bare hands, then followed the thread out of the maze to safety.

15th-century zodiac sign for Sagittarius

CENTAURS AND THE MINOTAUR IN BOOKS AND FILMS

📖 *Shadow of the Minotaur*
Alan Gibbons

📖 *The Horse and His Boy*
C S Lewis

📖 *Jason and the Gorgon's Blood*
Jane Yolen

🎥 *Fantasia* (1940)

🎥 *The Lion, the Witch and the Wardrobe* (2005)

Riddles and prophecies

For thousands of years people have wanted to understand the world, and to look at the end of the story and discover their own destiny. The more they search, the more mysteries they find. Oracles and wise men often speak in riddles, so that those who hear must work to understand. The Sphinx of Thebes used riddles as a trap, and the Great Sphinx of Giza is a riddle in himself.

The Delphic oracle's mysterious words were translated by priests — and sometimes misunderstood. When King Croesus (died c.546BCE) asked if he should invade Persia (modern-day Iran), she said that if he did, a mighty empire would fall. Expecting victory, he invaded — but it was his own empire that was destroyed.

ORACLES

An oracle has the ability to see into the future and to speak words of wisdom to those who seek information.

The oracle at Delphi, Greece, is one of the most famous. Here, within the temple of Apollo, the Greek god of prophecy, was a narrow opening through which vapours rose from deep within the earth. Inside, on a tripod above the fissure, sat the oracle herself, in a trance. She was consulted by kings and warriors, who gave great wealth to the shrine.

Crystal balls — globes of quartz crystal as clear as glass — have long been believed to have magical properties. Traditionally, a crystal ball is used for scrying — seeing the future. Some claim to see images of what is to come in the glass; others say that gazing into the crystal focuses the psychic powers, and that the visions the fortune-teller sees are actually in the mind.

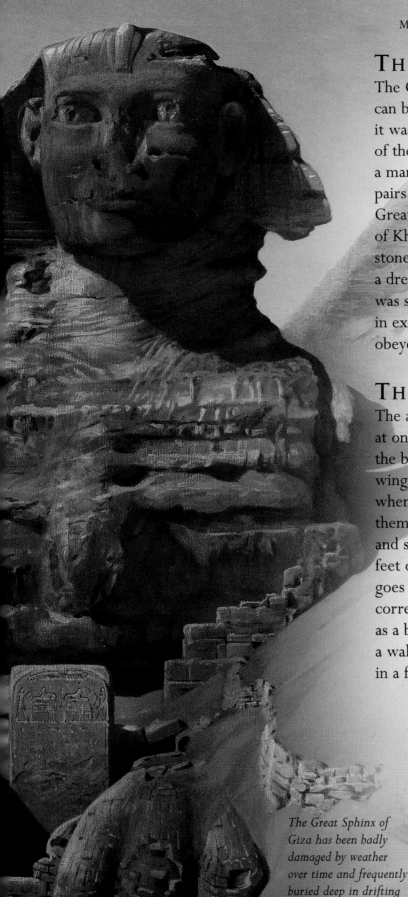

THE GREAT SPHINX OF GIZA

The Great Sphinx still keeps his secrets. No one can be certain who made him or when – though it was at least 4,500 years ago. He is carved out of the limestone bedrock, with a lion's body and a man's head. Other Egyptian sphinxes are set in pairs or rows, guarding temples and tombs, but the Great Sphinx stands alone near the great Pyramid of Khafre. According to the inscription on the stone slab between his paws, he appeared in a dream to Thutmose IV (b.1425BCE) when he was still a prince, asking him to clear the sand in exchange for the kingship of Egypt. Thutmose obeyed and the sphinx kept his part of the bargain.

THE SPHINX OF THEBES

The ancient city of Thebes in Upper Egypt was at one time stalked by a monstrous sphinx with the body of a lion, the head of a woman and huge wings. She asked riddles of passing travellers – and when they gave the wrong answer, she devoured them. At last, a man named Oedipus approached and she set him this riddle: 'What goes on four feet on two feet and three, but the more feet it goes on the weaker it be?' Oedipus gave the correct answer: 'A man – he crawls on all fours as a baby, walks on two feet as an adult and uses a walking stick in old age.' The sphinx killed herself in a fury and Oedipus was crowned king of Thebes.

The Great Sphinx of Giza has been badly damaged by weather over time and frequently buried deep in drifting sand. The sacred cobra on his forehead shows that he is royal.

RIDDLES AND PROPHECIES IN BOOKS AND FILMS

📖 *The Oracle Betrayed*
Catherine Fisher

📖 *Northern Lights*
Philip Pullman

📖 *The Hobbit*
J R R Tolkien

🎬 *The Dark Crystal* (1982)

Giants in the land

In British folklore, Gog and Magog are two giants who protect the city of London and whose likenesses have been carried in the annual Lord Mayor's procession since the reign of King Henry V (1387–1422).

*I*n the creation myths of many civilizations, the giants are the earliest beings. They are the massive forces of chaos and nature. Sometimes they built the mountains; sometimes their bodies formed the mountains. In ancient Greece, the Titans were the giant children of Gaea the Earth and Uranus the Sky. When the gods were born, the Titans fought with them, but were defeated.

ATLAS

Atlas was the leader of the Titans, and possibly king of the legendary land of Atlantis. During the great war between the gods and Titans, Atlas stormed the gods' stronghold of Mount Olympus. When the gods eventually triumphed, the Titans were banished, all except Atlas who was sentenced to carry the skies on his shoulders for all eternity. When Perseus flew past him, carrying the head of the Gorgon Medusa, Atlas was turned to stone. He is now the Atlas mountains, in northwest Africa.

Atlas is usually shown supporting the earth rather than the sky. In 1595, the Flemish map-maker Mercator produced the first modern collection of maps of the world, with a picture of Atlas at the front, and that is how books of maps came to be called atlases.

SHAPING THE LANDSCAPE

The huge Asilky of Russia piled up the mountains
and scooped out riverbeds and lakes but, like
the Titans, they threatened the gods and were
destroyed. The frost giants of Scandinavia
carved out valleys and mountain ranges,
and their melting bodies formed rivers.

Many of the giants fought, hurling enormous
stones at each other. This explains ancient upright
stones, sometimes standing in rows or in circles,
and also huge rocks lying many miles from where
they were formed. However, there are other
explanations – that prehistoric people put up
the standing stones and that glaciers carried the
rocks across the landscape during the Ice Age.

GIANT KILLERS

Fairy-tale giants are huge and strong, but also stupid and
easily outwitted. Jack the Giant Killer defeated one with
a simple trick. He challenged the giant to an eating contest,
concealing a bag under his clothes. As the giant ate, Jack
slipped his own food into the bag. As the giant's stomach
filled and swelled, so Jack's seemed to swell also. At last,
saying he needed to make more space, Jack plunged his
knife into the bag and let food spill out. The giant seized
his own knife, copied Jack's action – and killed himself.

GIANTS IN BOOKS AND FILMS

📖 *The BFG*
Roald Dahl

📖 *The Selfish Giant*
Oscar Wilde

🎥 *Harry Potter and the Chamber
of Secrets* (2002)

🎥 *The Iron Giant* (1999)

🎥 *Jack and the Beanstalk –
The Real Story* (2001)

🎥 *The Princess Bride* (1987)

Ogres and trolls

Giants may be either good or bad, but ogres are always bad and dangerous. It is thought that the word 'ogre' was first used by Charles Perrault in his collection of fairy tales published in France in CE1697. An English translation was published in the early 18th century, under the title Mother Goose Tales. Scandinavian trolls are also extremely dangerous and, like ogres, they enjoy eating human flesh.

THE CYCLOPS

The first group of one-eyed giants called Cyclops were, like the Titans, the children of Gaea and Uranus. Cyclops were blacksmiths who forged the thunderbolts of the great god Zeus (the Roman god Jupiter) and the trident of Poseidon (the Roman Neptune). Their forges burned in the hearts of volcanoes and the sound of their hammering shook the earth. Their human brides gave birth to the second group of giants, who lived as shepherds, herding flocks of giant sheep. A Cyclops imprisoned the ancient Greek hero Odysseus, together with all Odysseus' men, in his cavern. The Cyclops ate some of them and promised to devour the rest later. To escape, Odysseus used a sharpened stake to blind the Cyclops while he slept. When the enraged giant drove his sheep out to graze, he checked that his prisoners were not riding them to freedom – but did not guess they were clinging to the wool on the sheep's undersides.

TROLLS

The trolls of Scandinavian myth (right)
are enormous creatures, hideously ugly,
extremely strong and thoroughly evil-
minded. They live in caves, hiding deep
inside by day and lumbering out at
night to hunt. Their prey includes
humans. The best defence is to run
fast enough to lure them far from
their underground homes so they
are outside when the sun rises,
because exposure to sunlight
turns them to stone. The trows
of the Shetland Islands are similar
creatures, whose ancestors
arrived with the Viking invaders.

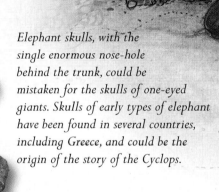

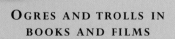

*Elephant skulls, with the
single enormous nose-hole
behind the trunk, could be
mistaken for the skulls of one-eyed
giants. Skulls of early types of elephant
have been found in several countries,
including Greece, and could be the
origin of the story of the Cyclops.*

OGRES AND TROLLS IN BOOKS AND FILMS

📖 *Sea of Trolls*
Nancy Farmer

📖 *Troll Fell*
Katherine Langrish

📖 *The Hobbit*
J R R Tolkien

🎥 *The Goonies* (1985)

🎥 *Shrek* (2001)

THE WINDIGO

The Windigo is a native American ogre-like
creature, who is also a shape-shifter. He
is an evil spirit who roams the forests and
wilderness of southern Canada, in search
of human meat. The Windigo can take the
form of a giant timber-wolf, but often he is
seen as a man, tall as a mighty tree, who
travels in blizzards so that he cannot easily
be seen. He has great strength and speed, and
can let out a scream so terrifying that his
victim is paralysed with fear and unable to
run. He has something in common with a
werewolf because anyone who is bitten but
escapes will inevitably become a Windigo.

Sea-beings

Our distant ancestors came from the sea and the memory remains in our salty blood and tears. It has such a hold on us, is so vast and mysterious, that it is easy to believe it is as much the home of the gods as the shifting sky or the shadowy underworld. Every civilization had its sea gods, riding the waves and raising or calming storms. Perhaps the greatest of these is Poseidon.

The word 'trident' means three-toothed. It is a three-pronged staff used by fishermen in Greece and wielded by the sea god known as Poseidon or Neptune. In the Christian belief, it is carried by the devil and used to torment sinners.

POSEIDON (NEPTUNE)

The powerful Greek god Poseidon is known as Neptune in Roman mythology. He rules the sea from his palace of coral and gemstones, just as Zeus rules the sky from Mount Olympus, and Hades governs the underworld. The earth is shared between the three. Poseidon has the power to create earthquakes, storms and shipwrecks by striking the ground with his trident. If he is in a good mood, though, he will calm the seas, which is why sailors try never to offend him.

The hippocampus is part-dolphin and part-horse, a massive creature that draws the chariot of Poseidon, but the name is also given to the tiny, delicate pipe-fish known as a sea-horse.

The conch is a sea creature, whose shell can become a kind of bugle when the animal is removed and the tip broken away to form a mouthpiece. The Hindu god Vishnu used a conch, and it is still used in Hindu religious ceremonies, including weddings. The Triton's horn conch, the largest of its kind, can reach 40cm in length.

SEA-BEINGS IN BOOKS AND FILMS

📖 ***The Sea Fairies***
L Frank Baum

📖 ***Harry Potter and the Goblet of Fire***
J K Rowling

📖 ***Nicholas Pipe***
Robert D San Souci

📖 ***The Missing Link***
Kate Thompson

🎥 ***The Little Mermaid***
(1989)

TRITON AND THE TRITONS

The first Triton was the son of Poseidon and Amphitrite, one of the Nereids. Half-man and half-fish, his fish-tail is forked and his body covered in scales. He uses the largest of the conch shells – known as the Tritons' trumpet – as a horn. There are many other Tritons, both male and female. All blow on conch shells and have forked fish-tails, and some – the centaur-tritons – also have the front legs of horses. They are wild and noisy and escort the chariots of the sea gods. In the sky, the largest moon of the planet Neptune has been named Triton.

THE HALF-WAY PEOPLE

The First Nation tribes of Canada, who spend much of the summer sea-fishing, are just one of many groups with stories of the half-way people, half-men and half-fish, who raise storms if angered. Japan has the Ningyo – not a human with a fish-tail but a fish with a human head – and descriptions of the ugly Margyr of Greenland make it sound like a walrus. It seems likely that a number of reported sightings have been of other species – walrus, seal, dugong and manatee – all of which will raise their heads out of the water to stare at passing boats. Certainly, many reports suggest that mer-men and mer-women are not older relatives of mermaids but creatures of a different race.

Mermaids

*I*n the days when vessels were powered by oarsmen or by wind
in their sails, mermaids were sometimes described
as looking strange, with animal rather than
human heads. They have grown more handsome
with time and now are as pretty as nymphs
with fish-tails. Like the Sirens, they have
wonderful singing voices, and they share
with the seal women the possibility
of bearing children to mortal men.

THE LORE OF MERMAIDS

The image of a lovely fish-tailed woman,
sitting on a rock gazing into a mirror
and combing her long hair, is familiar,
and her story starts at least as far
back as ancient Babylon.

The mermaid is sometimes said to
be the fantasy of men too long at sea
in a time when a voyage could last
years. Yet a group of divers off the
coast of Hawaii saw a mermaid as
recently as 1998. Or maybe the
mermaid is actually a Siren,
(see page 72) carrying not a
mirror but a lyre (the ancient
stringed instrument of the
Sirens) and not a comb but a
plectrum to pluck its strings.

Possibly the mermaid is as
real as a dolphin. Or maybe
she is a spirit of the sea and as
beautiful and dangerous as
the ocean she lives in.

This fake mermaid is from Aden, Yemen. Such deceptions are known as Jenny Hanivers — though no one is sure where the name originated. The fake creatures are made from parts of other animals.

It has always been believed that mermaids can foretell the future, so perhaps they sing not to lure ships onto rocks, but to warn of a coming storm.

SEAL WOMEN

Seal women, called selkies in the Orkney Islands, are known in remote areas where seals come ashore to give birth to their pups. It is said that every ninth night the seals take off their skins and become human. They prefer not to be seen, but it has happened more than once that a man watching secretly has fallen in love with a seal woman. In each case, he has stolen and hidden her seal-skin, forcing her to remain in human form after which he marries her and has children and a happy life with her. In each case, too, the seal woman has eventually found her seal-skin, put it on, and slipped back into the sea never to be seen again. There are still families today whose ancestors claim descent from such a marriage.

MERMAIDS IN BOOKS AND FILMS

📖 *The Litle Mermaid*
Hans Christian Andersen

📖 *Half-Human*
Bruce Coville

📖 *Wet Magic*
E Nesbit

🎥 *The Secret of Roan Inish* (1994)

🎥 *Splash* (1984)

6

Magic and spells

Magic is an ancient art, practised by wizards, witches, sorcerers and their kind. These powerful people can use their knowledge for good or evil. They may work with many devices, including spells, which can be a single word or several, often chanted as part of a ritual, and used in different ways — to protect or damage; to alter or make invisible; to see or change the future.

Witches and wise women

Witches, perhaps surprisingly, can be male or female.
There are evil witches who follow the devil and wish
to do harm, and good witches who are followers of
the pagan religion Wicca, the Old English word for 'witch'.
Wise women are knowledgeable about natural forces and
living things — their skills could seem almost supernatural.
The witches of fantasy can behave like all or any of these.

WARLOCKS

A dangerous male witch is a warlock.
The word comes from the Old English
war loga, meaning 'liar' or 'deceiver',
and is used for one who has sold his soul
to that great liar and deceiver, the devil.
Male witches who are interested only
in healing, rain-making, and encouraging
plants to grow and animals to thrive
are not warlocks.

WICCA

Modern Wicca began in the late 1930s,
but its followers look back to the beliefs
of the ancient Egyptians and the early
Celts. They believe in an earth goddess
and the horned god, Cernunnos,
sometimes called Herne the Hunter
(see page 36), who has no connection
with the devil. Wiccans believe that
whatever a person does returns at
three times the strength. Therefore,
all Wiccan magic is intended to do
good, because a harmful spell
would be certain to backfire.

**WITCHES AND WISE WOMEN
IN BOOKS AND FILMS**

📖 *The Spook's Apprentice*
Joseph Delaney

📖 *The Worst Witch*
Jill Murphy

📖 *The Wee Free Men*
Terry Pratchett

🎥 *Hocus Pocus* (1993)

🎥 *Willow* (1988)

🎥 *The Witches* (1990)

---

*Many witches can shape-
shift, usually choosing
to become animals, often
cats or hares. If a witch
is injured while in
hare-form, he or she
will have the same
injury when back
in human form.*

THE POWERS OF WITCHES

Witches are not usually born with magical powers but must gain them, by learning, by experimenting or, it is said, by begging them from the devil himself. However, they can be born with natural abilities, and the seventh son of a seventh son, or the seventh daughter of a seventh daughter, will have an instinctive talent for spellcraft.

The idea that most witches work for the devil is widespread, but some say it is untrue — a misunderstanding by the early Christian church, which was responsible for torturing and even burning alive those suspected of witchcraft from the 4th century CE to the 18th century.

The medieval ducking stool was one way of testing if someone was a witch. The suspect was strapped into the chair, which was then submerged in the water. A witch would survive — and then be killed. Anyone who drowned was declared innocent — and also dead.

WITCH MARKS

Witches who worked for the devil were said to carry marks on their bodies as a kind of seal of their pact with him. A witch mark could be a mole, a freckle, a scar or a birthmark — all common features that might be found on any person. If a woman, however innocent, was accused of witchcraft, she was examined, and any mark on her body was pronounced a witch's mark and a certain sign of her guilt.

Female witches are not always old and ugly, they can be young and beautiful, like this one seen dancing with demons.

Famous witches and enchantresses

Enchantresses have something in common with elves — they are always born with their powers already within them. Few are wholly human, and the enchantress-goddess Circe has no mortal blood in her at all. Witches are usually human, and their powers are the gifts of dark forces or the result of study and experiment. However, the most eminent of the witches, Hecate, is purely a supernatural being.

CIRCE

Circe (left), the daughter of the Greek sun god Helios, lives on an island. When sailors are lured ashore by her singing, which is as beautiful as that of the Sirens, she uses her enchantment to turn them into animals. Long ago, she transformed the crew of Odysseus into pigs but, with the help of Hermes, Odysseus compelled her to return them to human form. Circe fell in love with him, persuaded him to stay for a year and, before he left, taught him how to save himself and his men from the songs of the Sirens and the dangers of Scylla and Charybdis (see pages 72–73).

Baba Yaga with mortar and pestle – and a birch broom to sweep away her tracks.

BABA YAGA

Baba Yaga is a horrifying Russian cannibal witch. Her favourite victims are children. She likes to cook and eat them, and crunch on their bones. She lives deep in the Russian forest, in a little hut that spins around on chickens' legs, surrounded by a fence made of human skulls on spikes. She travels in a mortar – a type of bowl used for grinding herbs – and paddles her way through the air with a pestle, which is the instrument used to grind the herbs. Wherever Baba Yaga flies, terrible storms and tempests follow.

MORGAN LE FAY

Stories of Morgan le Fay, or Morgana, are written in Celtic mythology and in the tales of King Arthur, legendary King of Britain. She is sometimes described as the fairy queen of the magical land of Avalon, occasionally as a river goddess, often as Arthur's sister, and sometimes as the Morrigan (see pages 124–125). She is a frightening and cruel figure who, according to some legends, tried to kill Arthur and to frighten his queen, Guinevere, to death.

HECATE

The queen of the witches and a goddess of the underworld, Hecate is a figure of darkness who haunts graveyards and awakens phantoms to terrify the living. She is a triple goddess, and in pictures and statues she usually has three faces, and sometimes three joined bodies as well. The faces may be human, showing her as young, middle-aged and very old. Sometimes, though, one face is of a woman, one a dog and one a horse.

This mask of Rangda, the evil witch goddess of Indonesian mythology, is carried in Balinese ceremonial dances.

FAMOUS WITCHES AND ENCHANTRESSES IN BOOKS

☐ *The Castle of Llyr*
Lloyd Alexander

☐ *The Dream Stealer*
Gregory Maguire

☐ *Winter of the Ice Wizard*
Mary Pope Osborne

☐ *Old Peter's Russian Tales*
Arthur Ransome

Spells, cauldrons and familiars

Certain things have been associated with witches for centuries, especially the witches of Europe and North America. They are the witches' equipment, used for flying, brewing potions and working their craft. As well as their knowledge of magic, witches share with wizards their understanding of spells. There are thousands of possible spells, varying greatly in strength and purpose — and, like any power, they can be used for good or ill.

BROOMSTICKS

The belief that witches can fly is ancient and widespread. The traditional witch's broom, or besom, was for centuries the standard household brush, used by most people to sweep their floors. Witches fly, but they have no wings so they must have something to ride on to carry them through the sky. Almost all witches operated from their own homes and, as a broom was always handy, it became their chosen vehicle.

CAULDRONS

Originally, cauldrons were nothing more sinister than large, rounded pots that stood or hung over a hearth fire to cook food. Just as a witch would use whatever was to hand to ride on, so the domestic cauldron was used to brew bewitching mixtures, among them love potions and brews designed to poison, heal or make invisible.

Medieval pictures show witches on brooms, and even male witches riding pitchforks. Both brooms and pitchforks were common in countryside homes.

FAMILIARS

The witches of fantasy, whether good or evil, are often accompanied by animal familiars, usually cats. In medieval times, it was believed all witches worked for the devil, and it was he who provided the familiar, a demon in animal form, to carry messages between him and the witch. This familiar might be an owl, a toad or a goat, but was most often a cat. So, during the years when witches were hunted, innocent old women with pet cats were at serious risk.

WITCHES' HATS

Only witches in Europe and North America wear pointed hats; in other continents they have long, wild hair or headscarves. One possible explanation is that in 16th-century CE England many countrywomen wore pointed hats, and the fashion may have lingered among the rural wonder-working women, who healed the ills of humans and animals. Another is that the early Quakers wore similar hats, and in the late 17th century many were falsely accused of witchcraft. Finally, it may be that the pointed hat was actually a cone of power (see page 96).

Even when most households had cookers and saucepans with handles, the witch of fantasy continued to use her traditional cooking pot in which to create her various magical brews.

SPELLS, CAULDRONS AND FAMILIARS IN BOOKS AND FILMS

📖 *Northern Lights*
Philip Pullman

📖 *Harry Potter and the Philosopher's Stone*
J K Rowling

📖 *Gobbolino the Witch's Cat*
Ursula Moray Williams

🎥 *Bedknobs and Broomsticks* (1971)

🎥 *Kiki's Delivery Service* (1989)

Notable wizards

There are many famous wizard-magicians in fantasy, in history, and in myths and legends. Often the tales of their lives and works have changed in the telling, over the centuries, until it is no longer possible to discover where and how they began. Some, such as John Dee, were human; others, such as Merlin, were only part-human; and Gwydion and Hermes Trismegistus may have been entirely supernatural beings.

JOHN DEE

An astrologer, mathematician, alchemist and student of the occult, John Dee (1527–1608) was highly educated, and was so clever with conjuring tricks that some thought he was in league with the devil. At one time, he was accused of witchcraft. However, he became adviser and secret diplomatic agent to Queen Elizabeth I and, during her reign, he was safe from persecution. Although he once claimed he had succeeded in transforming common metal into gold, he died a poor man.

MERLIN

The stories that surround the great wizard Merlin (left) are as many and as complex as the spells he wove. It is said he had a human mother, but his father was a demon from whom he inherited the gift of prophesy. His studies of magic were deep, and he is credited with, among other things, causing some of the huge rocks from which Stonehenge was built to travel all the way from Wales. However, Merlin was baptized and he never used sorcery or black magic. He is probably best known as the wise guide and teacher of King Arthur.

POWER OF NAMES

Sorcerers and witches are not th[...]
to understand the importance of [...]
elves know it too. Possessing a p[...]
name is essential to gaining powe[...]
or her. It is unwise to allow a wo[...]
magic to know your true name –[...]
be given only to those who are tr[...]
trustworthy. This works both [...]

Little People are usually ca[...]
their real names secret [...]

GWYDION

Gwydion was a wise, powerful and knowledgeable Welsh wizard of Celtic mythology. His magical powers were strong, and he was a poet as well as a messenger of the gods, like the Greek Hermes and the Roman Mercury.

Stonehenge is a prehistoric monument on Salisbury Plain in Wiltshire, England. At dawn on Midsummer Day, the sun strikes the altar stone – it is thought the whole structure was used as a giant calendar to chart the sun's progress through the sky.

Hermes Trismegistus is said to have been the first alchemist, whose knowledge was greater than that of all the rest together.

NOTABLE WIZARDS IN BOOKS AND FILMS

📖 *The Seeing Stone*
Kevin Crossley-Holland

📖 *Welsh Legends and Folk Tales*
Gwyn Jones

📖 *The Once and Future King*
T H White

🎬 *Merlin* (1998)

🎬 *The Sword in the Stone* (1963)

HERMES TRISMEGISTUS

Hermes Trismegistus, whose name means 'three times as great as Hermes', was a magician, a mystic, an alchemist and an astrologer whose collected writings are known as the *Hermetica*. He is said to have all the powers of Hermes, the Greek messenger of the gods and lord of magic, and also of Thoth, the Egyptian god of wisdom and magic. He may have been a mythical figure, or possibly there was a series of wizards and alchemists who used this name, and perhaps the writings of the *Hermetica* are the work of many.

Sorcerers a

Sorcerers and i
Their magic i
It is risky to
worship the devil o
all power for thems
strike a bargain wi
word for 'corpse', a
who calls up the de

SORCERY
All workers of magic are
kind of power; the powe
future, to heal, to harm
events. Many intend to u
for good ends. Those wh
though, desire total and
Sorcery is not fundamen
good or evil; it is about
a power so mighty it can
very stars in the sky. Sor
attempting to rule the u

Amulets, talismans and charms

Traditionally, an amulet is a magical object that already contains power within itself. A talisman is an object that has had its power put into it from outside. A charm is spoken or written and, if written, may be in words or in symbols. As time has passed, the meanings have become blurred, and the words used interchangeably. Then again, a magical object can be given extra power by the addition of a charm, and so can be all three at once.

The Eye of Horus is a powerful amulet or charm against most kinds of evil, but especially the evil eye – a malevolent glance from a being with magical powers. Horus was the falcon-headed god of the ancient Egyptians.

SCARABS
The scarab is one of the most powerful of ancient Egyptian amulets. The scarab is a beetle with beautiful, iridescent wing cases. It feeds on animal dung, which it first rolls into a ball. Also, the female lays her egg within a buried dung-ball. The egg hatches, the grub grows and changes to emerge as an adult beetle, as if born from the earth. So the scarab is an emblem of resurrection (coming back to life). It is also a symbol of the sun because it is said to roll the ball from east to west, in imitation of the sun and the route of Ra, the Egyptian sun god.

Other cultures recognize power in different objects. Amulets are made from peach wood or peach stones in China. In Africa, the wood of a sacred tree is used. People in many countries over most centuries credit crystals with healing properties. Even a stone, shaped and smoothed by water, especially if found in a sacred place, can be judged to be magical.

In New Zealand, Maories carve Tikis out of jade to represent protective spirits, which are also called Tikis.

LODESTONES

A lodestone is a naturally magnetic piece of rock containing iron ore, also known as magnetite. It attracts iron and, if suspended or balanced so it can move, will point to the magnetic poles of the earth. Its name comes from the Old English word *lod*, meaning 'way' – so it is a way-stone, an early form of compass. It is said to bestow strength and determination, and to protect from all harm. Alexander the Great had lodestone amulets issued to each of his soldiers.

AMULETS, TALISMANS AND CHARMS IN BOOKS AND FILMS

📖 *The Story of the Amulet*
E Nesbit

📖 *The Amulet of Samarkand*
Jonathan Stroud

🎥 *Dungeons & Dragons* (2000)

🎥 *The Golden Voyage of Sinbad* (1974)

A dried scarab beetle or a man-made likeness (opposite page, top left), is believed to bring fortune and health to the living and, when placed in a tomb, eternal life to the dead. The scarab's likeness is shaped in many materials, including gold and precious stones. Often a prayer or charm is scratched on the underside.

Two wizards, locked in battle, may shape-shift many times, each trying to turn into the stronger or more cunning species.

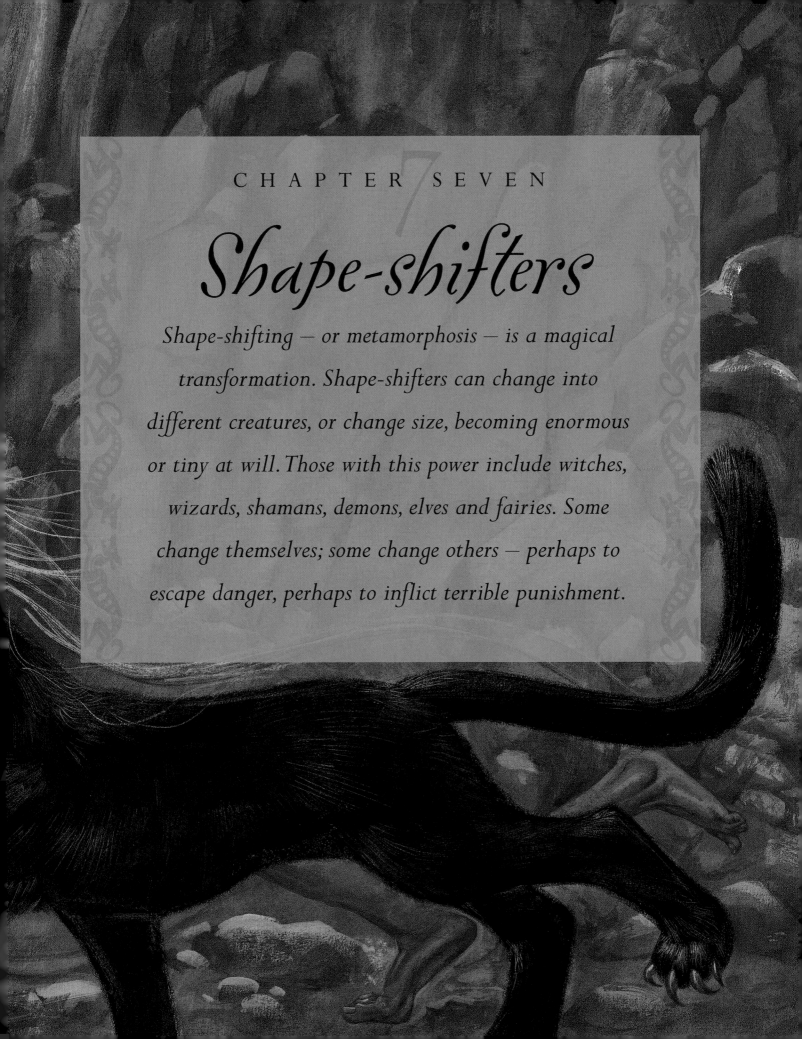

Shape-shifters

Shape-shifting — or metamorphosis — is a magical transformation. Shape-shifters can change into different creatures, or change size, becoming enormous or tiny at will. Those with this power include witches, wizards, shamans, demons, elves and fairies. Some change themselves; some change others — perhaps to escape danger, perhaps to inflict terrible punishment.

Werewolves

The werewolf is possibly the most dramatic, terrifying and famous of all shape-shifters. He is known throughout northern Europe, North America and Canada. In fact, he is known wherever wolf packs lived in the past or live now. Even in countries where the wolf has become extinct, the werewolf still raises his muzzle to the moon and howls. Other countries and other cultures have other were-creatures — South America has the werejaguar, China the weresnake, Africa and Australia the werecrocodile and India the weretiger.

THE POWER OF WOLVES

Wolves are brave and loyal to their pack. They are good mothers, and not only to their own kind. There have been several cases of female wolves suckling and caring for abandoned human infants. Even so, wolves are fierce, especially when they are hungry, and will easily make a meal of a child or lone adult. In the past, when most houses had flimsy wooden walls, a pack could easily break its way in. If the occupants had no guns, they had no way of protecting themselves. In such times, the wolf seemed supernaturally powerful. Stories of shape-shifters were widespread and it was a small step to the horrifying belief that a man – with his knowledge of people's homes, lives and weaknesses – could become an even more deadly form of wolf.

In 1858, the Baroness Dudevant (better known as the French novelist George Sand) told her son about her sighting of a group of werewolves. Maurice, who also used the surname Sand, drew this picture from her description.

108

GWYDION

Gwydion was a wise, powerful and knowledgeable Welsh wizard of Celtic mythology. His magical powers were strong, and he was a poet as well as a messenger of the gods, like the Greek Hermes and the Roman Mercury.

Stonehenge is a prehistoric monument on Salisbury Plain in Wiltshire, England. At dawn on Midsummer Day, the sun strikes the altar stone — it is thought the whole structure was used as a giant calendar to chart the sun's progress through the sky.

Hermes Trismegistus is said to have been the first alchemist, whose knowledge was greater than that of all the rest together.

NOTABLE WIZARDS IN BOOKS AND FILMS

📖 *The Seeing Stone*
Kevin Crossley-Holland

📖 *Welsh Legends and Folk Tales*
Gwyn Jones

📖 *The Once and Future King*
T H White

🎥 *Merlin* (1998)

🎥 *The Sword in the Stone* (1963)

HERMES TRISMEGISTUS

Hermes Trismegistus, whose name means 'three times as great as Hermes', was a magician, a mystic, an alchemist and an astrologer whose collected writings are known as the *Hermetica*. He is said to have all the powers of Hermes, the Greek messenger of the gods and lord of magic, and also of Thoth, the Egyptian god of wisdom and magic. He may have been a mythical figure, or possibly there was a series of wizards and alchemists who used this name, and perhaps the writings of the *Hermetica* are the work of many.

Sorcerers and necromancers

Sorcerers and necromancers are practitioners of the dark arts. Their magic is rarely benevolent and usually dangerous. It is risky to seek help from either. Sorcerers do not worship the devil or indeed anyone because they want all power for themselves. However, they may seek to strike a bargain with him. Necro is the Greek word for 'corpse', and a necromancer is one who calls up the dead as assistants.

A grimoire is a sorcerer's handbook, containing recipes for potions, instructions for rituals, and designs for magical symbols and images. They are rare and ancient, often written in code because at many times in many countries magic was illegal, and often punishable by death.

SORCERY

All workers of magic are seeking some kind of power; the power to foretell the future, to heal, to harm or to influence events. Many intend to use their power for good ends. Those who practise sorcery, though, desire total and absolute power. Sorcery is not fundamentally about doing good or evil; it is about developing a power so mighty it can influence the very stars in the sky. Sorcery is about attempting to rule the universe.

NECROMANCY

The art of raising the dead and compelling them to assist in enchantment or the casting of spells is called necromancy. It may be used by many magic-workers, including sorcerers and witches. It is a perilous craft because a demon may answer the summons instead of the chosen dead, or the dead may be angry to be disturbed.

POWER OF NAMES

Sorcerers and witches are not the only ones to understand the importance of names, the elves know it too. Possessing a person's true name is essential to gaining power over him or her. It is unwise to allow a worker of magic to know your true name — it should be given only to those who are trusted and trustworthy. This works both ways, and the Little People are usually careful to keep their real names secret from humans.

The five-pointed star of a pentagram

SORCERERS AND NECROMANCERS IN BOOKS AND FILMS

- *The High King*
  Lloyd Alexander

- *The Farthest Shore*
  Ursula K Le Guin

- *Sabriel*
  Garth Nix

- *Shadowmancer*
  G P Taylor

- *The Black Cauldron* (1985)

MAGIC CIRCLES AND SQUARES

A magic circle protects the sorcerer or magician who stands within it, because demons and spirits can enter only if invited. A magic square is a device for creating magic and calling up spirits. The designs used are precise and elaborate, their positioning is crucial, and complex rituals accompany their construction.

The pentagram is one of the best-known magic symbols. *Penta* means 'five' and a pentagram is a five-pointed star with the single point at the top. It is sometimes called a pentacle, but in fact a pentacle is any magic symbol or pattern.

The so-called Hand of Glory is a dried or mummified human hand, used as a candleholder by sorcerers and necromancers. It is supposed to have the ability to paralyse all who see it so that they cannot move, speak or run away.

101

Portals and rings

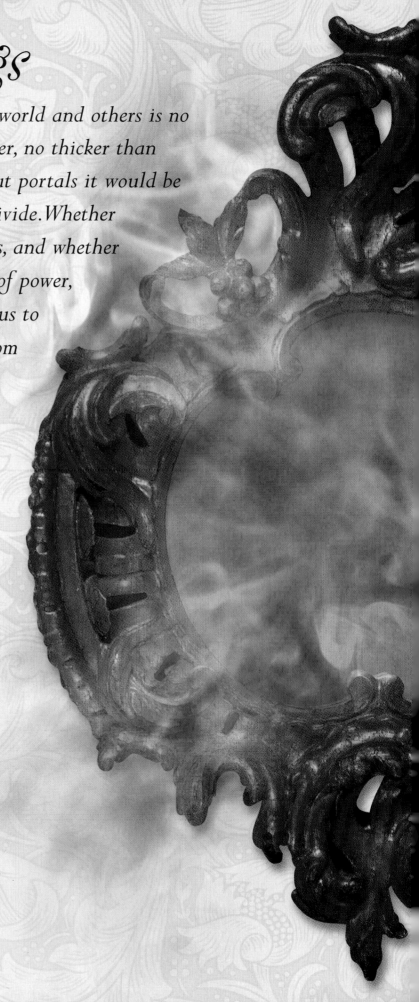

The division between our world and others is no wider than a cat's whisker, no thicker than a spider's web. Yet without portals it would be impossible to pass through the divide. Whether they are called doors or gateways, and whether opened by magic words or rings of power, portals are two-way — allowing us to enter other worlds and beings from other worlds to slip into ours.

MIRRORS

The moment in *Alice Through the Looking Glass*, in which Alice steps through the soft, misty surface of a huge mirror into a different world is echoed in other tales of fantasy, some far older and some newer.

The mirrors of fantasy have many uses. As well as portals, they can be the means of gaining information. The magic mirror that will answer questions — including 'Who is the fairest of them all?' in the story *Snow White and the Seven Dwarfs* — is well known. They can also offer revelations and a sure way of checking if a visitor is a vampire or a werewolf — these creatures cast no reflection.

A mirror need not be a traditional sheet of glass, silvered on the back for a clear reflection, or be one of the metal mirrors of antiquity. It can be any reflecting surface — a puddle, pond, lake, crystal or highly polished shield.

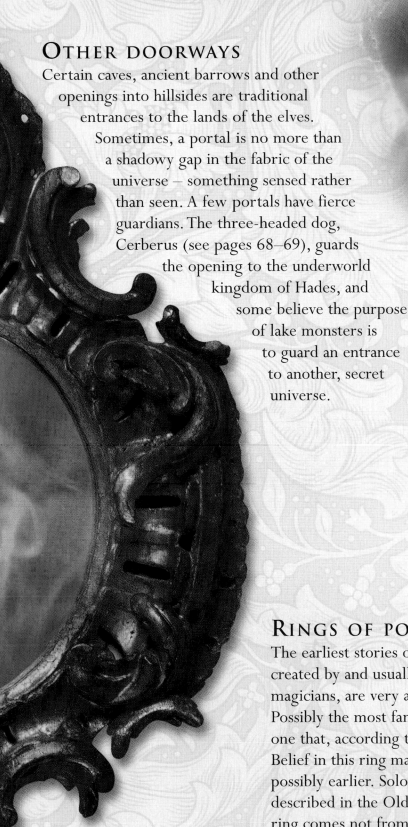

OTHER DOORWAYS

Certain caves, ancient barrows and other openings into hillsides are traditional entrances to the lands of the elves. Sometimes, a portal is no more than a shadowy gap in the fabric of the universe – something sensed rather than seen. A few portals have fierce guardians. The three-headed dog, Cerberus (see pages 68–69), guards the opening to the underworld kingdom of Hades, and some believe the purpose of lake monsters is to guard an entrance to another, secret universe.

PORTALS AND RINGS IN BOOKS AND FILMS

📖 *Alice Through the Looking Glass*
Lewis Carroll

📖 *The Lion, the Witch and the Wardrobe*
C S Lewis

📖 *The Lord of the Rings*
J R R Tolkien

🎥 *Harry Potter and the Philosopher's Stone* (2001)

🎥 *Snow White and the Seven Dwarfs* (1937)

RINGS OF POWER

The earliest stories of rings of power, created by and usually owned by magicians, are very ancient indeed. Possibly the most famous of these rings is the one that, according to legend, was owned by King Solomon. Belief in this ring may date back to the 4th century CE, possibly earlier. Solomon was the great and wise king of Israel, described in the Old Testament, but the story of the magic ring comes not from the Bible but from elsewhere. Legend says he used it when building the Temple of Jerusalem in order to gain power over the demons who tried to destroy it.

Since then there have been many tales of rings that contained the power to control demons, humans and other beings – or to unlock the portals into other worlds.

Amulets, talismans and charms

Traditionally, an amulet is a magical object that already contains power within itself. A talisman is an object that has had its power put into it from outside. A charm is spoken or written and, if written, may be in words or in symbols. As time has passed, the meanings have become blurred, and the words used interchangeably. Then again, a magical object can be given extra power by the addition of a charm, and so can be all three at once.

The Eye of Horus is a powerful amulet or charm against most kinds of evil, but especially the evil eye — a malevolent glance from a being with magical powers. Horus was the falcon-headed god of the ancient Egyptians.

SCARABS

The scarab is one of the most powerful of ancient Egyptian amulets. The scarab is a beetle with beautiful, iridescent wing cases. It feeds on animal dung, which it first rolls into a ball. Also, the female lays her egg within a buried dung-ball. The egg hatches, the grub grows and changes to emerge as an adult beetle, as if born from the earth. So the scarab is an emblem of resurrection (coming back to life). It is also a symbol of the sun because it is said to roll the ball from east to west, in imitation of the sun and the route of Ra, the Egyptian sun god.

Other cultures recognize power in different objects. Amulets are made from peach wood or peach stones in China. In Africa, the wood of a sacred tree is used. People in many countries over most centuries credit crystals with healing properties. Even a stone, shaped and smoothed by water, especially if found in a sacred place, can be judged to be magical.

In New Zealand, Maories carve Tikis out of jade to represent protective spirits, which are also called Tikis.

LODESTONES

A lodestone is a naturally magnetic piece of rock containing iron ore, also known as magnetite. It attracts iron and, if suspended or balanced so it can move, will point to the magnetic poles of the earth. Its name comes from the Old English word *lod*, meaning 'way' – so it is a way-stone, an early form of compass. It is said to bestow strength and determination, and to protect from all harm. Alexander the Great had lodestone amulets issued to each of his soldiers.

AMULETS, TALISMANS AND CHARMS IN BOOKS AND FILMS

📖 ***The Story of the Amulet***
E Nesbit

📖 ***The Amulet of Samarkand***
Jonathan Stroud

🎥 ***Dungeons & Dragons*** (2000)

🎥 ***The Golden Voyage of Sinbad*** (1974)

A dried scarab beetle or a man-made likeness (opposite page, top left), is believed to bring fortune and health to the living and, when placed in a tomb, eternal life to the dead. The scarab's likeness is shaped in many materials, including gold and precious stones. Often a prayer or charm is scratched on the underside.

Two wizards, locked in battle, may shape-shift many times, each trying to turn into the stronger or more cunning species.

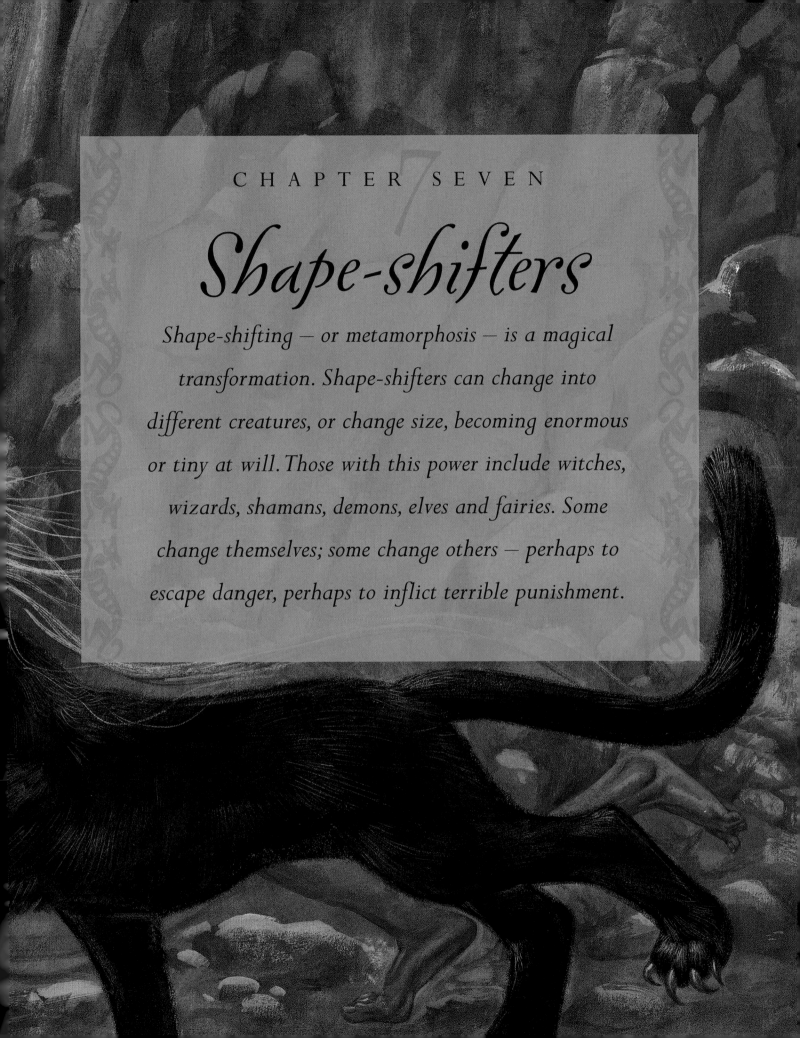

Shape-shifters

Shape-shifting — or metamorphosis — is a magical transformation. Shape-shifters can change into different creatures, or change size, becoming enormous or tiny at will. Those with this power include witches, wizards, shamans, demons, elves and fairies. Some change themselves; some change others — perhaps to escape danger, perhaps to inflict terrible punishment.

Werewolves

The werewolf is possibly the most dramatic, terrifying and famous of all shape-shifters. He is known throughout northern Europe, North America and Canada. In fact, he is known wherever wolf packs lived in the past or live now. Even in countries where the wolf has become extinct, the werewolf still raises his muzzle to the moon and howls. Other countries and other cultures have other were-creatures — South America has the werejaguar, China the weresnake, Africa and Australia the werecrocodile and India the weretiger.

THE POWER OF WOLVES

Wolves are brave and loyal to their pack. They are good mothers, and not only to their own kind. There have been several cases of female wolves suckling and caring for abandoned human infants. Even so, wolves are fierce, especially when they are hungry, and will easily make a meal of a child or lone adult. In the past, when most houses had flimsy wooden walls, a pack could easily break its way in. If the occupants had no guns, they had no way of protecting themselves. In such times, the wolf seemed supernaturally powerful. Stories of shape-shifters were widespread and it was a small step to the horrifying belief that a man — with his knowledge of people's homes, lives and weaknesses — could become an even more deadly form of wolf.

In 1858, the Baroness Dudevant (better known as the French novelist George Sand) told her son about her sighting of a group of werewolves. Maurice, who also used the surname Sand, drew this picture from her description.

SILVER BULLETS

In the time of the pagan wolf cults, the wolf-man was often gentle and wise. The werewolf of fantasy, though, is always a ravening beast, who will rip its victim's throat out with its strong jaws. The change from human to wolf takes place at full moon, traditionally a time of magic and madness.

A man (and they usually are men) may become a werewolf because one has bitten him. It could be because he has used a magic ointment or has put on a wolf's pelt to change himself. Or it may be because he has been bewitched. If bewitched, he will return to human form after nine years, provided he has not eaten human flesh in that time. When faced with a werewolf, the most effective weapons are iron or silver — the most convenient is a silver-tipped arrow or a silver bullet. The creature will always revert to its human shape as it dies.

WEREWOLVES IN BOOKS AND FILMS

- *The Wereling*
  Stephen Cole

- *The Wolving Time*
  Patrick Jennings

- *The Golem's Eye*
  Jonathan Stroud

- *The 10th Kingdom* (2000)

- *Harry Potter and the Prisoner of Azkaban* (2004)

Wer *is Old English for 'man', so werewolf (sometimes spelt werwolf) is a man-wolf. For a man to become a wolf, almost every part of the body must change. His hair and claws grow, and teeth become larger and stronger. The head changes shape and develops a muzzle. The back becomes longer, shoulders flatten, and legs and arms reshape their very bones.*

Sometimes, in the past, people were
accidentally buried alive (something
which could not happen with modern
medical techniques). If an opened grave
revealed a corpse whose struggles to
escape had left blood on mouth and
fingernails, it was declared a vampire.

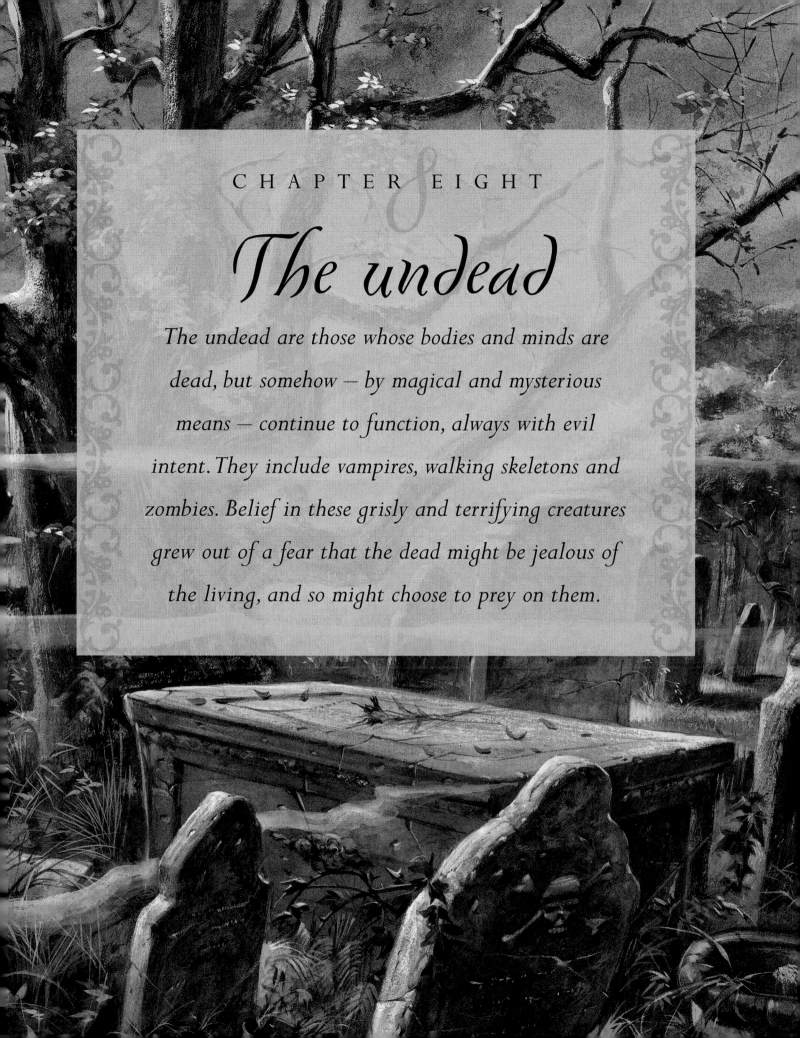

The undead

The undead are those whose bodies and minds are dead, but somehow — by magical and mysterious means — continue to function, always with evil intent. They include vampires, walking skeletons and zombies. Belief in these grisly and terrifying creatures grew out of a fear that the dead might be jealous of the living, and so might choose to prey on them.

Vampires

Vampire bats live in Central and South America and the West Indies. They make tiny incisions in the skin of their victims with their sharp teeth and then lap, rather than suck, the blood. Their animal or human victims never turn into bats or vampires.

Vampires are as old as recorded history. They are creatures of the night — blood-sucking shape-shifters who can change into smoke, mist, bats, wolves, dogs or cats. In Japan, it is the vampire cat of Nabeshima who is most feared. Female vampires in India linger at crossroads to suck the blood of elephants. Vampire legends come from China, Egypt, Greece, Malaysia, Africa, the Americas, Arabia and, perhaps especially, eastern Europe.

As dawn breaks, vampires must climb back into the safety of their coffins. During the daylight hours, vampires are vulnerable to attack by those who wish to destroy them.

EASTERN EUROPEAN VAMPIRES

Vampir is a Magyar, or Hungarian, word for 'undead', and similar words are used in many eastern European languages. Another title is Nosferatu, which means 'living corpse'. Vampires cast no shadow and have no reflection. Folklore describes them as red-faced and unshaven, with loud voices, ever-open mouths and pronounced canine teeth, or fangs. It also says they leap on their victims and crush and smother them while sucking their blood. The pale, elegant, clean-shaven vampire – such as Count Dracula – who leaves two neat holes in a victim's neck did not appear until the l9th century CE.

The common way to become a vampire is to be bitten by one, just as the surest way to become a werewolf is from a bite. In fact, vampires are closely related to werewolves and they often have wolves and bats in their power.

The two-tailed vampire cat of Nabeshima, in Japan, kills by strangling, not biting. Her story tells that she murdered a princess, shape-shifted to look like her, and then preyed on the prince. Eventually, she was caught and killed.

DEFENCE AGAINST VAMPIRES

Traditionally, a vampire can cross the threshold only if invited – so the first line of defence is to close the door on one.

Garlic, the bulb of a plant of the onion family, often used in cooking, has been relied upon for centuries to ward off evil of all kinds, especially vampires. Medically, eating garlic can help prevent the blood from clotting, and you might think vampires would find this appealing in a victim, but they do not. Iron and, to a lesser extent, silver are also deterrents. Vampires are active only between sunset and sunrise, so the daylight hours are safe. During those daylight hours they have to return to their coffins to rest. Finding the coffin and destroying both it and the vampire inside will bring the reign of terror to an end, but it is a messy business. Recommended methods are to drive a stake through the vampire's heart, or to behead it, or to burn the body. Some say all three are necessary, others that any one of them will do the trick.

Count Dracula

In CE1897, a book was published that changed people's ideas about vampires forever. Dracula, by the Irish author Bram (Abraham) Stoker, is not the earliest vampire story, but it is by far the most famous and the most influential. Other 19th century authors wrote about pale and aristocratic vampires, but Bram Stoker's elegantly dressed count fixed this image in the collective imagination, and confirmed the belief that the human vampire is able to shape-shift at will into a bat.

Most of Count Dracula's victims were young and beautiful women who, once bitten, were doomed to become vampires themselves.

DRACULA

In Bram Stoker's Gothic horror story, Count Dracula buys an ancient estate in Britain. A young solicitor called Jonathan Harker, whose diaries tell the story, travels to the count's castle in Transylvania to arrange matters. Among other dreadful experiences, he discovers the count resting by day in his coffin in a ruined chapel. The count sails for Whitby in Yorkshire, to his new estate, taking his coffin and boxes of earth from the Dracula family graveyard with him. None of the crew survives the voyage. In England, Harker and Professor van Helsing, an authority on vampires who recognizes the true nature of Dracula, struggle – with partial success – to save Harker's fiancée and her best friend from the count's vampirish ways. Eventually, they pursue him back to Transylvania where they at last succeed in beheading him and stabbing him through the heart – at which point he turns to dust.

This portrait of Vlad Dracula was painted by a German artist in the 16th century CE. Vlad ruled Wallachia from 1456–1462, during which he earned the legendary name, Vlad the Impaler, through a reign of terror.

VLAD THE IMPALER

Dracula once existed, although he was not a vampire. He was born in CE1430, son of Prince Vlad of Wallachia. Wallachia is in the southern part of Romania, not all that far from Transylvania. Vlad was a member of the distinguished Hungarian Order of the Dragon, and became known as Vlad Dracul, or Vlad the Dragon. In Wallachian, the words for dragon and devil are the same, and as Vlad was a cruel ruler the name was appropriate. The name Dracula means young, or junior, Dracul, so Vlad's son became Vlad Dracula. Worse even than his father, he was also called Vlad the Impaler because, it is said, he caused more than 100,000 people to be impaled on sharpened stakes as a form of execution.

The true story is the source of many elements of the novel – the name, the country, the cruelty and the sharpened stakes, although in the story the sharpened stakes are used against the 'devil', not by him.

COUNT DRACULA IN BOOKS

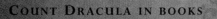

📖 ***Vlad the Drac***
Ann Jungman

📖 ***Dracula's Tomb***
Colin McNaughton

📖 ***Dracula's Revenge***
Gary Morecambe

📖 ***Dracula***
Mike Stocks

Skeletons and symbolic heads

Reverence for the head, detached from its body, goes back to the earliest civilizations. Real heads have been trophies of war, sources of wisdom and protectors of realms. Heads carved from wood or stone are found in almost every country. Skeletons, though, are symbols of death. To cultures that dread death, skeletons and skulls are always frightening. Skulls are especially eerie — and have even been used as macabre drinking cups.

SCREAMING SKULLS

Most stories of screaming skulls come from England. Usually, the skull is in a large house and has been handed down through generations — it might belong to an ancestor of the family, or, more chillingly, a murder victim or an executed murderer. If anyone moves it to another site, or even gives it a decent burial, the following night will be shattered by unearthly screams, and the skull will be discovered back in its usual place at daybreak.

This is a mask showing the Aztec creator god Tezcatlipoca, whose name means 'smoking mirror'. It was made in Mexico in the 15th or 16th century CE from a human skull decorated with turquoise mosaic.

SYMBOLIC HEADS

To those who believed the head contained the spirit, even after death, the taking of a head was a way of claiming some of the energy and power of the owner. Generations ago, head-hunting was a regular practice in Amazonia, New Guinea, India, the Philippines and the Solomon Islands. The Jivaro, a fierce people of Ecuador, shrunk the severed heads of their opponents to trap their souls and prevent them from taking revenge.

Bran the Blessed, a great mythic king of Britain, ordered that his head be buried in the White Hill in London, where the Tower of London now stands, to protect against invaders. It is rumoured to have been removed to a safer, secret place by King Arthur, but Bran's sacred birds, the ravens, still live at the Tower and protect the country.

SKELETONS AND SYMBOLIC HEADS IN BOOKS AND FILMS

📖 *Charlie Eggleston's Talking Skull*
Bruce Coville

📖 *How I Got My Shrunken Head*
R L Stine

📖 *The Crystal Skulls*
Jan Visser

🎥 *Jason and the Argonauts* (1963)

🎥 *Vice Versa* (1988)

THE DAY OF THE DEAD

Skeletons are not always frightening or sinister. On the Mexican Day of the Dead – *Dia de los Muertos* – there are fantasy images of death and skeletons everywhere, but it is a happy occasion. It is a massive family reunion to honour the benevolent dead, ancestors and friends who are gone but not forgotten. Personal altars hold their images, surrounded by the things they loved in life. There are candles everywhere, and also marigolds – the flowers of the dead. The festival goes back to 3,500 BCE, though its ancient traditions blended with Christianity when the Spanish conquistadors arrived in the 16th century CE. Although it begins on 31 October, it is far older than Hallowe'en and quite separate from it.

Skulls, such as this one, are made of sugar for children to eat during the Mexican Day of the Dead.

117

Mummies, zombies and golems

In fantasy, zombies and golems are powered by a magician who controls them from a distance, often with evil intent. Mummies are powered by their own anger towards those who have disturbed their tombs. All are strong and terrifying. It is impossible to reason with them and impossible to kill them — mummies and zombies because they are already dead, and golems because they were never truly alive.

MUMMIES

The preserved body of a human or animal is called a mummy. Bodies can be preserved naturally in ice or desert sand, but several early civilizations deliberately preserved their dead. They removed the internal organs, protected the skin with oils, and bound the body with cloths. The most famous were the ancient Egyptians. Their royal families and priests were mummified, placed in beautiful coffins with protective amulets, and then buried in elaborate tombs or pyramids, with supplies of food, drink and valuables for the afterlife. For centuries, despite stories of ancient curses, the buried treasure attracted thieves. Also, curiosity about ancient Egypt tempted archaeologists to enter pyramids, remove and examine whatever they found and, usually, place it in museums.

Stories of vengeful mummies attacking the living are almost certainly born out of the guilt of those who have robbed and disrespected them.

ZOMBIES

A sorcerer creates a zombie by re-animating a corpse, which is then used to threaten or attack his or her victims. The first zombies were in Haiti, a part of the Haitian voodoo cult. Later, zombies loomed out of the misty imaginary lands. None of them has any will of their own. Supposedly, if they eat salty food or look at the sea, they will return to their graves.

GOLEMS

A golem (below) is a man-figure made of mud or clay, activated by spells and by a special word written either on its forehead or on a parchment placed in its mouth. One of the words used is *emeth*, meaning 'life'. When the word is removed, it collapses – on at least one occasion crushing its master. The most famous golem-maker, according to legend, was the Rabbi of Prague, Judah Loew ben Bezaleel (1525–1609). He used a golem as a servant, but always carefully rested it on a Friday so it would be still during the Sabbath (Saturday). One day he forgot, and only just had time to stop it by removing the parchment from the golem's mouth as it plodded towards the synagogue. The figure turned to dust and its remains are said to lie in the synagogue's attic.

Ghosts and spirits

Ghosts arise from different sources. Some are the earthbound souls of those who do not realize they are dead, or who have unfinished business in the world of the living. A few are evil wraiths or mischievous poltergeists. Many are harmless place-memories in which a past event is replayed. Spirits are a different order of being, with no physical body unless they choose to wear one to become visible.

Jinn or genii

The jinn who drifted into the world of fantasy through The Thousand And One Nights, *often known as* The Arabian Nights, *are very different to the jinn of Islam. These tales were told by Indian, Persian and Arabian storytellers for many hundreds of years. They were first written down around CE850 in Arabic, reaching Europe in French translation in the early 18th century. Since then, they have appeared in many languages.*

This painting shows Sinbad the sailor over-awed by the enormous genie he has released from its imprisoning jar.

THE NAMES OF THE JINN

In Arabic, they are jinn or djinn in the plural and jinni or djinni in the singular. In French and English, they are usually genii in the plural and genie in the singular. These are all names for the same creatures, which are created from fire and can take any shape they choose — animal or human — and can be of any size, including gigantic and awe-inspiring. It is said that most are hostile, though some can be friendly. It is possible for magicians or wise men and women to gain power over jinn and use them to perform amazing and magical tasks. Like the Little People, though, even friendly jinn can be unpredictable, and certainly anyone who breaks an agreement with jinn will live to regret it.

In all there are five different types. The least powerful is the jann, next come the jinn (which is also the overall name for all five), and then the sheytans, or devils. The afrits, sometimes called efreets, are very powerful, but the marids are the most powerful and dangerous of all.

THE LAMP AND THE BOTTLES

Magicians have trapped jinn in various ways. In the story *Aladdin and his Wonderful Lamp* — which was probably a late addition to *The Arabian Nights* collection — a jinni was imprisoned in an old brass lamp (like this one, right). Rubbing the lamp released the jinni, and it would obey whoever set it free.

Traditionally, it is said that the great and wise King Solomon shut misbehaving jinn in lead-stoppered bottles and threw them into the sea. Sometimes these were caught in fishing nets. Any person who opened a bottle might be granted three wishes or, more likely, would find the freed spirit so dangerous it was wiser to trick it into re-entering the bottle, which could be closed securely and thrown back.

Traditionally, King Solomon's flying carpet could carry his whole court, but most were just like any beautiful hand-woven rug until powered into flight by magic.

JINN OR GENII IN BOOKS AND FILMS

📖 *The Twelve and the Genii*
Pauline Clarke

📖 *The Akhenaten Adventure*
P B Kerr

📖 *The Amulet of Samarkand*
Jonathan Stroud

🎥 *Aladdin* (1992)

🎥 *Arabian Nights* (2000)

Messengers of death

Death is a mystery that has been solved in different ways by the religions, mythologies and fantasies of every civilization. One of the ideas found in the most ancient stories, and still believed by many today, is that the moment when the Fates cut the thread of a life can be foreseen. If the time of death can be known, then it follows that a death messenger may bring a warning.

The washerwoman at the ford is called the Bean Nighe in Gaelic. She is found in the lands of the Celts, crouching by a ford or pool, washing the clothes of those whose death is near. If a passing mortal asks politely, she will tell the names of the chosen.

THE FETCH

The fetch is a living ghost, the wraith-like image of a person who is soon to die. It may be seen by relations or close friends or by the person him- or herself. In the dark of night it appears only as a small flame, known as a fetch light, and may be confused with other phantom lights.

In Irish tradition, the fetch only foretells death if it appears at night. If a fetch is seen in the morning, it predicts a long life.

MESSENGERS OF DEATH IN BOOKS

📖 *The Weirdstone of Brisingamen*
Alan Garner

📖 *The Hounds of the Morrigan*
Pat O'Shea

📖 *Halloween Pie*
Michael O Tunnell

📖 *Harry Potter and the Prisoner of Azkaban*
J K Rowling

THE BANSHEE

Her name comes from the Gaelic
Bean Sidhe, meaning 'a woman of the
fairies' or 'a female spirit'. Her wailing
voice is heard when death is near. Each
banshee is attached to an Irish family or
clan, and cries only for one of her own.
Traditionally, her keening is heard around
the ancestral home, even if the one who
is dying is far away, and the sound indicates
the type of death — low and soft
for peaceful passing, harsh and high
for a violent end. It is also said that
only aristocratic families have banshees,
and a person of lowly birth who hears
a banshee's lament has nothing to fear.

DOPPELGÄNGERS

The name doppelgänger means 'double-
goer' in German, more often translated
as double-walker or co-walker. Like the
fetch, it is an exact replica of a specific
human being, and it is usually believed
that to see one's own doppelgänger
is to receive warning that
death is close. Certainly
the French writer
Guy de Maupassant
(1850–1893) said he saw
his doppelgänger towards
the end of his life, and it
is said that both Queen Elizabeth I
(1533–1603) and the English poet
Shelley (1792–1822) saw theirs shortly
before their deaths. However, there are
cases where — either because of a wrinkle
in time or because some people are
able to project images of themselves —
a doppelgänger has been seen by several
people, yet the person it represents
has continued to live for many years.

*The Morrigan is the great queen of the Tuatha
Dé Danaan, the ancient Irish gods whose descendants
are the Little People. She is a shape-shifter — sometimes
a beautiful warrior goddess, sometimes a wolf or a crow. On
the field of battle, she is a shrieking, ancient hag, leaping
around the killing fields, choosing which soldiers shall die.*

Ghouls and evil spirits

Ghouls are ancient creatures of horror and
fantasy. They share with other evil spirits —
including boggarts, goblins, imps, wights
and the mara — a desire to bring terror and danger
to human beings. Traditionally, they can be kept
at bay by silver, by the sound of bells and by
a refusal to allow the mind to be ruled by fear.

*Traditionally, the ringing
of church bells will drive
away storms, plagues,
demons, ghouls, and
all other ill winds and
dangerous creatures.*

GHÛLS AND GHOULS

In Arabic folklore, a ghûl is a monstrous, shape-shifting demon.
It may take the form of a dog or hyena (below) to open graves
and feast on the bodies within. It also feeds on lost, lone
travellers. In European fantasy, ghouls are among the undead,
one-time humans who have become as they are by eating
human flesh. They are hideous and give off a stench of rotting
carrion. Though very strong, they are not intelligent and it is
easier for a human to outwit
them than fight them.

NIGHTMARES

The mares of the night are not female horses but demons known in Norse and Old English as mara or mera. They crouch on a sleeper's chest and bring bad dreams, originally called nightmaras or, in German, *alpdrücken*. At first, the word described only dreams of crushing or suffocation; since the early 19th century, it has been used for any bad or frightening dream.

An evil imp is in the service of the devil. His greatest skill is spreading lies to create anxiety and confusion. His most powerful weapon is fear itself.

Nightmares can be caused by guilt. Here, Ivan IV, who was crowned Tsar (Emperor) of Russia in 1547, is visited by the angry ghosts of the men, women and children he murdered. He was a fierce ruler, often so cruel to his subjects that he became known as Ivan the Terrible.

GOBLINS, BOGGARTS AND IMPS

Boggarts and goblins are evil creatures that fall within the wide and varied group of elvish beings, called the Little People. Imps are rather different. Their name comes from an Old English word meaning 'young shoot', especially one that can be cut and used to grow a new plant. It can be used affectionately for a mischievous child, but in fantasy it usually means an offshoot of the devil himself.

WIGHTS

Wight comes from an Anglo-Saxon word *wiht*, which had several meanings, including 'person' and 'thing'. It was sometimes used to refer to the spirit guardians of sacred places, who were called landvættir, or land-wights, in Norse mythology. Originally, they commanded respect rather than fear, but in more recent times they have been regarded as evil, especially since J R R Tolkien wrote of the terrible barrow-wights in *The Lord of the Rings*.

GHOULS AND EVIL SPIRITS IN BOOKS AND FILMS

📖 ***One Thousand and One Nights***
Geraldine McCaughrean

📖 ***The Book of Nightmares***
John Peel

📖 ***The Lord of the Rings***
J R R Tolkien

🎥 ***Harry Potter and the Prisoner of Azkaban*** (2004)

Ghosts and hauntings

A ghost is the spirit of a living creature that has died. It haunts the place most used during life, or the site of a single dramatic event — usually death. Unlike spirit-beings, such as djinn, a ghost has limited range — a room, a house, a pathway, or a specific corner of a field or wood. It is almost unheard of for a ghost to move elsewhere or follow a living person. Ghosts really belong in another dimension and there is always a reason why they have remained in ours.

GENTLE GHOSTS

Some ghosts are anxious to reassure those left behind that they still love them. Some bring warnings of danger or try to show the location of something important — a will, perhaps. Some simply do not understand they are dead and try to carry on as before. These ghosts have unfinished business, and cannot rest until everything has been resolved.

The Korean dokkaebi is unlike any of these. He has a human shape, though only one leg, a hairy body, staring eyes, sharp teeth and long finger and toe nails. Despite his startling appearance, and habit of haunting graveyards and old houses, he is playful, humorous and harmless.

DRAMATIC HAUNTINGS

Many of the most frightening hauntings are by those who have been hanged, murdered, tortured or walled up alive for their beliefs. Some may be place memories, but some are ghosts trapped at the site of their death by their own rage against the living who caused their suffering. These, too, have unfinished business, and may be laid to rest if their bones are found and buried decently and their stories told.

PLACE-MEMORY AND TIME-SLIP

Certain places can 'remember' or record events that have often been repeated. No one knows how or where the sights, and sometimes sounds, are recorded – in the fabric of buildings or in the rocks below the earth's surface – nor what causes them to replay.

Time-slip is when either the human witness slips back into the past or else a moment from the past slips into the present. A brief vision of an ancient army on the march in the present-day world could be place-memory. If, however, the visible world around the ancient army changes so that it, too, belongs to the distant past, the likely explanation is time-slip.

Time-slip is rare, and the human observer is warned not to try to change the past. Place-memory is not uncommon, and the observer has no more power to change or affect anything than he or she could have on a film.

GHOSTS IN BOOKS AND FILMS

📖 *A Christmas Carol*
Charles Dickens

📖 *The Woman in Black*
Susan Hill

📖 *Macbeth*
William Shakespeare, Andrew Matthews

📖 *The Canterville Ghost*
Oscar Wilde

🎥 *Casper* (1995)

🎥 *Ghostbusters* (1984)

Poltergeists

A poltergeist is not an ordinary ghost but a form of energy – sometimes very violent energy. It seems likely that there is more than one type, and more than one cause. Poltergeist activity has been recorded all over the world for at least 2,000 years. It has been studied for several hundred years, most recently using high-powered electronic equipment, yet still no one can claim to understand it fully.

POLTERGEIST ACTIVITY

An ordinary ghost can be terrifying, but a poltergeist can also be dangerous because it has physical power. Its name comes from the German *poltern*, which means 'to create a disturbance' and *geist*, which means 'ghost'. A poltergeist is always noisy and usually disruptive. It has kinetic energy – which means it can move things about. It can throw heavy objects across a room, smash china and glass, and even throw stones that were not in the room in the first place. A poltergeist's activities can be triggered anywhere at any time and, unless stopped, will build to a crescendo before dying down – and then perhaps beginning all over again.

A really active poltergeist can destroy everything within its range, and people who are nearby may be hit by flying furniture or cut by pieces of broken china or glass.

DEMONS AND LITTLE PEOPLE

Some poltergeists are aggressive; others are just mischievous and no more than a nuisance. In the world of fantasy, imps, demons and goblins all have the ability to throw things and create chaos, and most of the Little People, if they feel annoyed or slighted, can also cause strange noises and upheavals.

PSYCHOKINETIC ENERGY

A poltergeist almost always focuses on one person in a household and that person is usually, though not always, young. There is a possibility that the person central to the attacks may be causing them, accidentally or on purpose, using psychokinetic energy, or mind-power.

LEY LINES

In 1921, Alfred Watkins, a respected merchant and amateur archaeologist, noticed that stone circles, standing stones, megalithic tombs, churches built on ancient sacred sites, and beacon hills seemed to be placed in straight lines across the British countryside. He named them ley lines and assumed they marked prehistoric trading routes. It is possible, though, that they also mark the currents of earth energy which are known in other countries, and which in China are called *lung-mei*, or dragon paths. Research shows that poltergeist activity often occurs on ley lines, especially where leys cross each other.

POLTERGEISTS IN BOOKS AND FILMS

📖 *Eustace*
Catherine Jinks

📖 *The Ghost of Thomas Kempe*
Penelope Lively

📖 *Harry Potter and the Philosopher's Stone*
J K Rowling

🎥 *The Haunted Mansion* (2003)

🎥 *Ghostbusters* (1984)

Ghost ships and eerie beasts

Fully rigged sailing ships that come into view and then melt away and vanish, horses that emerge out of the night but are not really there, fierce black dogs that disappear as suddenly as they appear — all have been reported over the years, often by reliable witnesses. Some have been explained away as time-slip or place-memory (see page 129), as mirages or other tricks of the light. Others remain mysterious.

In Norse mythology, Fenrir the Fenris Wolf is a vast and aggressive creature. The gods protected themselves and the world by tying him down with a magic chain, from which he will not break free until the end of the world.

THE FLYING DUTCHMAN

The most famous of many phantom ships is known as *The Flying Dutchman* — although in fact 'Dutchman' refers to the captain, not the ship. It is a 17th-century two-masted brigantine, a Dutch merchant vessel. There are several legends attached to her, told in books, a film and a Wagner opera. All agree she ran into trouble in a storm off the Cape of Good Hope, South Africa. Most say her captain refused to turn back but swore to heaven and the devil that he would round the Cape if he had to sail until Doomsday. So the ghostly ship, with her crew of corpses and skeletons, sails on forever, a chilling omen of doom. Among those said to have seen her are a young midshipman in the Royal Navy who was to become King George V of Britain, and the crew of a World War II German U-boat.

St Elmo's Fire may account for some of the sightings of ghostly looking ships. This is a shimmering blue light that dances on the masts and superstructure of ships after electrical storms.

The Barguest occurs mainly in northern Britain. It is a terrible creature that haunts dark lanes and churchyards, most often in the form of a giant dog with eyes like burning coals, although it can shape-shift into a cat or a goblin.

THE DOGS OF DEATH

Many cultures connect dogs — whose association with humans goes back thousands of years — with death. They may guard the entrance to the underworld, like Cerberus, or guide the spirits of the dead, like Syama and Sabala (see pages 68–69). In many cultures, too, spectral black dogs are linked with individual families — and the sight of one heralds the death of a family member, in much the same way as the cry of the banshee. Ghostly hounds have been sighted on many a lonely path at night, especially in Britain and other Celtic lands, usually alone, occasionally hunting in packs. Even if they do not bring death they certainly arouse great fear.

Almost all animals are aware of the presence of ghosts and supernatural beings, but horses — long regarded as sacred animals — are especially sensitive. Most people who ride or work with them know that a horse can be 'spooked' by something that no one else can see.

The Wild Hunt

On winter nights of storm and fury, in the Celtic lands of northern Europe, the Wild and Savage Hunt can be heard — and may be glimpsed — streaming across the skies. The hooves of their phantom horses make the sound of thunder, their spectral hounds howl down the wind. The thousands of riders are the dead and the undead, seeking the souls of the damned. Sometimes the frenzied horses are black, accompanied by wild-eyed, jet-black hounds. Sometimes the horses are as pale as death and the red-eared hounds as white as snow. The fearsome hunt may be led by Odin or Woden, Norse god of death and magic, or by a spirit huntsman, or by the devil himself. If the huntsman is Gwyn ap Nuad, the Welsh god of war and death, the hounds will number only three — one white, one black and one blood red. Mortal dogs may howl as the hunt streams by, but mortal men and women should beware of looking at it for fear of being swept away.

THE WILD HUNT IN BOOKS

List of creatures by area

Some of the fantastic beings and creatures within this book are known almost everywhere. Some, though, seem to enter our own world only in specific countries or on specific continents. Then, too, certain magicians and monsters were born and lived (or still live) in one location. It is these that are listed here.

ARCTIC CIRCLE

uldra *Little People* (page 25)

GREENLAND:

Margyr *mythical being* (page 85)

AFRICA

camelopard *mysterious animal* (page 43)
werecrocodiles *shape-shifters* (page 108)

EGYPT:

Great Sphinx *mythical being* (page 79)
Hermes Trismegistus *wizard* (page 99)
mummies *the undead* (page 118)

SOUTH AFRICA:

Flying Dutchman *ghosts and spirits* (page 132)
Tokoloshi *Little People* (page 23)

THE AMERICAS

NORTH AMERICA:

bogeyman *Little People* (page 23)
Bokwus *nature spirit* (page 37)
Ogopogo (N'haitaka) *mysterious animal* Canada (page 46)
Sasquatch (Bigfoot) *mysterious animal* (page 45)
Slimy Slim *mysterious animal* USA (page 46)
Thunderbird *fabulous beast* (page 63)
Windigo *mythical being* (page 83)

CENTRAL AMERICA:

Quetzalcoatl *god and fabulous beast* (page 62)

SOUTH AMERICA:

Ahuitzotl *nature spirit* (page 38)
werejaguars *shape-shifters* (page 108)

ASIA

Arabian phoenix *fabulous beast* (page 61)
ghûls *shape-shifting demons* (page 126)
griffins *fabulous beasts* (pages 60–61)
jinn or **djinn** *ghosts and spirits* (pages 122–123)
Nagas and **Nagini** *gods and fabulous beasts* (page 67)
Roc *fabulous beast* (page 63)
Yeti (Abominable Snowman) *mysterious animal* (page 44)

CHINA:

Chinese dragon *fabulous beasts* (page 52)
Feng-Hwang *fabulous beasts* (page 61)
Ki Lin (Ch'i Lin) *fabulous beasts* (page 56)
weresnake *shape-shifter* (page 108)
Yellow Dragon *fabulous beasts* (page 53)

INDIA:

Garuda Bird *fabulous beast* (page 62)

manticore *mysterious animal* (page 42)
Syama the black and **Sabala the spotted** *fabulous beasts* (page 69)
weretigers *shape-shifters* (page 108)

INDONESIA:

Rangda *witch goddess* (page 93)

JAPAN:

Ho-o *fabulous beasts* (page 61)
Issie *mysterious animal* (page 46)
Japanese dragons *fabulous beasts* (page 52)
Kirin *fabulous beasts* (pages 56)
Ningyo *mythical being* (page 85)
vampire cat of Nabeshima *the undead* (page 112)

KOREA:

Korean dragons *fabulous beasts* (page 52)
dokkaebi *ghost* (page 128)

EUROPE

basilisk *fabulous animal* (page 65)
bluecaps *Little People* (page 24)
bogeymen *Little People* (page 23)
cockatrice *fabulous animal* (page 65)
doppelgängers *ghosts and spirits* (page 125)
ghouls *the undead* (page 126)
golems *clay monsters* (page 119)
Green Man *nature spirit* (page 37)
Hippogriff *fabulous beasts* (page 61)
Morgan le Fay *enchantress* (page 93)

Glossary

aggressive Hostile, warlike and liable to attack, with either words or weapons.

ancestors Great-grandparents, and their parents, and so on, all the way back to the distant past.

avengers Those who take revenge, often on behalf of others.

Aztecs Native American peoples who built a great empire in Mexico from the 14th century CE, until conquered by the Spanish in the 16th century.

barrows Ancient burial mounds.

benevolent Friendly, kindly or helpful.

billabongs Small rivers, or parts of rivers, that come to a dead end; stagnant pools.

cannibal A person or animal who eats the flesh of its own kind.

carrion Dead and rotten flesh.

celestial Of the sky, or the heavens.

composite Made up of several different parts.

constellation A group of stars, whose shape when seen from the earth seems to form the outline of beings or animals.

decomposing Decaying or rotting.

demons Evil spirits, devils.

destiny Fate, a future that has been planned in advance by the gods or some other power.

deterrent Anything that persuades someone against a certain course of action.

divine Like the gods, or coming from the gods, or God Himself.

dugong A large, air-breathing sea mammal related to the manatee. Both are sometimes called sea cows.

eerie Weird and frightening.

effigy Something made to look like, or represent, a person or god. An effigy may be made of almost any material, including stone, metal or clay.

elixir A liquid mixture, used to turn ordinary metal into gold, or as a medicine to give unusually long life to a patient.

emblem A symbol or a symbolic image, or picture of something.

enchantment A kind of magic.

eternity For ever and ever – time without end.

ethereal Light and delicate.

executed Killed, as a result of a sentence of death.

exposure To be uncovered or unprotected.

extinct Died out and no longer in existence.

fables Stories, sometimes supernatural, often with animal characters, told in order to teach a moral lesson. The word is sometimes used for myths and legends.

faery An ancient word for fairyland; also used to describe a being or creature who comes from fairyland.

ferocious Fierce and dangerous.

folklore The traditional beliefs of a people or culture, often containing memories of things that have actually happened in the distant past.

ford A part of a river or stream where the water is shallow enough for people, animals, carts or cars to cross.

foretell To tell about something before it has happened.

fossilized Preserved by nature in ice or dry sand, or turned into stone inside ancient rock. Fossilized remains are usually skeletons, or parts of skeletons, or plants – sometimes only the shape of the once-living creature or plant has been saved.

gauzy Being so thin and transparent that it is possible to see through to the other side.

gnarled Twisted and knobbly, like an old tree.

Gothic Gothic novels, such as Bram Stoker's *Dracula*, are always full of mystery, strange happenings and horror.

heraldry The decorations, symbols and colours used to represent a person, a family, or a ruler and his or her descendants. Originally used on banners, standards and shields so people could recognize each other in battle. Now used more widely, especially by cities and businesses.

hibernate To sleep through the winter.

hoard A store or collection of something.

hoaxes Fakes, imitations of a real thing, tricks or practical jokes.

humanity The human race.

immortal Living forever, never dying.

imperial Of an empire or emperor; royal.

instinctive Doing something by instinct, without thought or planning.

iridescent Glowing with rainbow colours, something which changes colour as it moves.

labyrinth A maze; pathways or passages that twist and turn, many leading to dead ends.

lance A weapon with a long wooden handle and a pointed tip.

legends Traditional stories, usually about a specific person or place. The word is sometimes used for myths and fables. Originally, all these stories were spoken not written. They were told by professional or amateur storytellers, or else passed down through families, and changed a little with every telling.

macabre Gruesome.

malicious Cruel, wanting to hurt and do harm.

martyr A person who suffers for his or her religious faith or beliefs, who is sometimes tortured or killed for refusing to give up these beliefs.

medieval Refers to the Middle Ages in Europe, from the 5th century to the middle of the 15th century CE.

meteorites Small pieces of rock or metal that fall to earth from outer space without burning up in the atmosphere. Meteorites that burn up and glow briefly in the night sky are called shooting stars.

mirages Optical illusions, things seen that are not really there.

mortal A human being who will, like all humans, eventually die.

myths Traditional stories, often about large subjects – the lives of gods and goddesses and the creation of this and other worlds. Many myths explain human behaviour and natural events, like earthquakes. The word is sometimes used for fables and legends.

navigation Finding the way, steering a ship, an aircraft, etc. on the right course.

navigator A person who is trained in navigation.

nourishing Giving energy and sustaining, or supporting, life. Usually used when talking of food.

occult To do with the supernatural and with mystical and magical knowledge.

omens Things that happen, or are seen, and are thought to predict the future.

outwitted To outwit someone, you need to be cleverer or craftier than they are.

pagan Not part of any of the main religions of the world, often following ancient beliefs and nature worship. Pagan does not mean Satanic or evil.

pestilence and plague Names for any kind of terrible disease that spreads rapidly and almost always kills its victims.

plectrum A small piece of horn, ivory, metal or plastic used to pluck the strings of a musical instrument such as a guitar or lute.

plesiosaurs Extinct dinosaurs with long necks and flippers that once lived in seas and lakes.

plumage The feathers of birds.

pollution Anything that makes the air, water or earth filthy, such as oil spills and smoke or gas pouring into the air.

provisions Food, water, milk and other supplies.

psychic Psychic events or happenings are mysterious and magical and cannot be explained or easily understood; a psychic is a person with occult powers.

putrid Rotten, rotted away, smelly and slimy.

realms Kingdoms, areas in the control of one ruler or group of rulers.

resurrection The return to life of someone who has died; rising from the dead.

revelations The revealing of knowledge; glimpses of the future, or of great truths.

rituals Ceremonial acts.

sacrificed Killed and offered to a god or gods.

shamans People who form a link between this world and the world of spirits. Sometimes, a type of priest.

shape-shift The ability to change from one shape into another – from man into wolf, for example.

shrine A sacred place, often decorated with sacred objects or pictures, where a god or saint is worshipped.

sonar Often used to search for things underwater; sound is sent out and its returning echoes are recorded on a screen, showing the shape of invisible underwater objects.

standards Flags or banners with colours, patterns or images that are easy to recognize and that represent a person or a group – a monarch, a kingdom, an army regiment or a noble family.

summons An order to appear.

supernatural Outside the normal laws of nature, mystical or magical; used of gods, ghosts and fairies, among others.

tempests Very bad storms with strong winds.

treacherous Not to be trusted, dangerous.

tribute A gift given to show respect.

U-boat A German submarine used in World War I and World War II.

vengeful Looking for vengeance or revenge.

venom A liquid poison produced by snakes and other reptiles, and injected into a victim with a bite or a sting.

vigorous Strong and energetic.

visions Things seen in the imagination or in dreams or trances.

voodoo A religion practised mainly in the Caribbean, especially Haiti.

wraith Ghost of a dead person.

Index

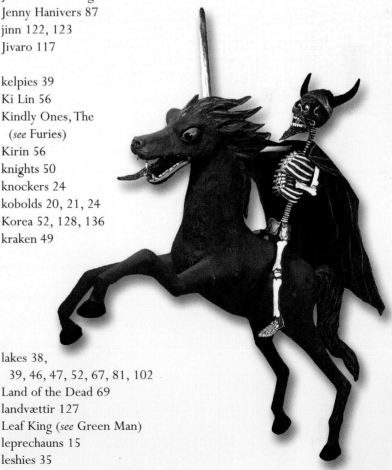

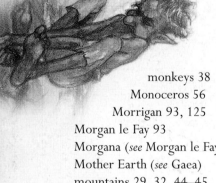

Acknowledgements

The publisher would like to thank the following for permission to reproduce their material. Every care has been taken to trace copyright holders. However, if there have been unintentional omissions or failure to trace copyright holders, we apologize and will, if informed, endeavour to make corrections in any future edition.

Key: *b* = bottom, *c* = centre, *l* = left, *r* = right, *t* = top

Cover: *front cover* Mark Turner/www.enchanted.co.uk/photography by Mark Eager/Runic Design; *cover flaps* Patricia Ludlow/Linden Artists; *back cover l* Topfoto; *back cover c* Popperfoto; *back cover r* Bridgeman Art Library (BAL)/The Marsden Archive

Pages: 1 Corbis/Elizabeth Whiting; 1*c* Corbis/State Russian Museum; 1*c* Corbis/Todd Gipstein; 1*c* Patricia Ludlow/Linden Artists; 2–3 John Howe/Arena; 4–5 John Howe/Arena; 5*tl* David Goode/www.david-goode.com; 6–7 Richard Hook/Linden Artists; 10–11 Nicki Palin;12–13 British Museum; 14 John Howe/Arena; 15*cl* BAL/Victoria & Albert Museum; 15*cr* Patricia Ludlow/Linden Artists; 16 Patricia Ludlow/Linden Artists; 17*tl* Corbis; 17*tl* Corbis/Buddy Mays; 17*c* Mary Evans Picture Library (MEPL); 18*tl* MEPL; 18*br* Topfoto; 19 BAL/Private Collection; 20 David Goode; 21*t* MEPL; 21*c* Patricia Ludlow/Linden Artists; 21*b* Patricia Ludlow/Linden Artists; 22*t* BAL/Fairy Art Museum, Tokyo; 22*b* David Goode; 22–23*c* Getty Imagebank; 23*tr* Bal/Private Collection; 24*tl* MEPL; 25 Richard Hook/Linden Artists; 26 David Goode; 27*b* Getty Hulton; 28–29 John Howe/Arena; 30 Corbis/Andrea Wells; 30*bl* Corbis/Christie's Images; 30–31 Corbis; 31*tr* Getty Imagebank; 32–33 Nicki Palin; 34*tl* Art Archive/Victoria & Albert Museum; 34*b* Topfoto; 35*bl* Getty Stone; 35*r* John Howe/Arena; 36*tl* BAL/ Private Collection; 36*bl* Topfoto; 36–37 John Howe/Arena; 38*cr* Werner Forman Archive; 38*bl* BAL/Private Collection; 39 Corbis/Corcoran Gallery of Art; 40*tl* Corbis; 40*r* Alamy; 41*tr* Mary Evans Picture Library; 41*cl* Getty Imagebank; 42–43 Richard Hook/Linden Artists; 44–45*t* Getty NGS; 44–45*b* Getty NGS; 44*t* Topfoto/Fortean; 44 Topfoto; 45*r* Lee Gibbons; 45*tr* Corbis/Darrell Guilin; 45*tr* Topfoto; 46 Popperfoto; 46–47 Patricia Ludlow/Linden Artists; 48–49 John Howe/Arena; 49 BAL/Fitzwilliam Museum, Cambridge; 50–51 John Howe/Arena; 52*tl* Corbis/Charles and Josette Lenars; 52–53 Corbis/Philadelphia Museum of Art; 54*tl* Corbis/Reuters; 54–55 John Howe/Arena; 55*tr* Corbis/National Gallery, London; 56*t* Kunsthistorische Museum, Vienna; 56*b* BAL/Musee National du Moyen Age, Cluny; 57 Nicki Palin; 58 Patricia Ludlow/Linden Artists; 59 BAL/Neue Pinatothek, Munich; 60–61 Getty Imagebank; 60–61 Corbis/Kevin Schaeffer; 60*b* Corbis/Araldo de Luca; 62*b* Corbis/Christie's Images; 62–63*t* Patricia Ludlow/Linden Artists; 63*b* Corbis; 64–65 Corbis Elio Ciol; 65*t* Nicki Palin; 66*br* BAL/Musee Gustave Moreau, Paris; 67 Corbis/Luca Tettoni; 68–69 Corbis/Tim Davis; 69 Art Archive/British Museum; 70–71 Scala/Vatican; 72*cl* BAL/National Gallery, Melbourne; 72–73 Getty Imagebank; 73*cl* Alamy; 73*tr* AKG, London; 74*bl* AKG, London; 74–75*c* Corbis/Araldo de Luca; 75*r* BAL/Felix Labisse Collection, France; 76 John Howe/Arena; 77*tl* BAL/Heraklion Museum, Crete; 77*br* Art Archive/Biblioteca Estense Modena/Dagli Orti; 78*tl* AKG, London; 78*bl* Alamy; 79 Corbis/Christie's Images; 80–81 Getty/RHPL; 80*tl* Art Archive/Real Biblioteca de lo Escorial/Dagli Orti; 80*br* Corbis; 81*tr* Mary Evans Picture Library; 82*l* BAL/Museum of Fine Arts, Boston; 82*lc* Corbis/Michael Prince; 83*cl* Natural History Museum, London; 83*tr* BAL/National Museum, Stockholm; 84–85 Michael Embden/Arena; 85*tl* BAL/Musee Conde, France; 87*tr* Topfoto; 88–89 John Howe/Arena; 90*bc* Alamy; 91*tr* AKG London; 91*b* John Howe/Arena; 92 John Howe/Arena; 93*tl* BAL; 93*cr* Werner Forman Archive; 94–95 BAL/Private Collection; 95*tr* BAL/Private Collection; 96*cl* BAL/de Morgan Centre, London; 96*br* BPK, Berlin/States Museum, Berlin; 97*c* Corbis; 97*br* Art Archive; 98 Julek Heller/Arena; 99*t* Topfoto; 99*c* Getty Imagebank; 100 Dominic Harman/Arena; 100–101*t* Art Archive/Dagli Orti; 100–101*b* Topfoto; 102–103 Corbis/Elizabeth Whiting; 102–103 Corbis/Russian State Museum; 103*tr* Getty Stone; 103*cr* Getty Photodisc Green; 104–105 Art Archive/Dagli Orti; 104*tl* Corbis/Gianni Dagli Orti; 104*cl, cr* Werner Forman Archive; 105*b* Science Photo Library; 106–107 Richard Hook/Linden Artists; 108–109 Getty Imagebank; 108*br* Topfoto; 110 Richard Hook/Linden Artists; 112*tl* Frank Lane Picture Agency; 112–113*b* Terry Oakes/Arena; 113*cl* Getty Imagebank; 113*cr* Getty Photodisc Green; 114–115 BAL/Marsden; 114*b* Les Edwards/Arena; 115*t* BAL; 116–117 British Museum; 116*b* British Museum; 117*c* Art Archive/Mexico City Museum; 117*b* British Museum; 118*both* Nicki Palin; 120–121 Dominic Harman/Arena; 122*l* BAL/Royal Watercolour Society; 123*c* Corbis/Hermann/Starke; 124*l* BAL/Musee d'Orsay; 125 Photolibrary.com/OSF; 126*tl* Getty Imagebank; 126*b* Getty Stone; 127*tl* BAL/Stavropol Museum, Russia; 127*cr* BAL/Detroit Institute of Arts; 128*r* Corbis/Olivier Martel; 128–129 Corbis/Sandro Vannini; 129*t* Corbis/Elizabeth Opalenik; 130*b* Corbis; 130–131*t* Corbis/Sandford Agliolo; 131*c* Photolibrary.com/OSF; 131*tr* Mary Evans Picture Library; 132–133 Corbis; 132*cl* Werner Forman Archive; 132–133 Corbis/Joseph Sohm; 133*t* Julek Heller/Arena; 134–135 BAL/Gavin Graham gallery; 138 Corbis/Christie's Images; 140 Mary Evans Picture Library; 141 British Museum; Patricia Ludlow/Linden Artists; 143 Nicki Palin

The book and film icons for the book panels on each spread: Encompass Graphics